OUTRÉ

Book One

Of

Deviation

Believe in The Possibility of Everything

~HORATIO PRESS

RG Adamson

Other Books

Admit to Mayhem, Lillian Dove Mystery

Cover designed by Karen Phillips

ISBN: 978-0-9903078-2-2

To

Joshua, Brendan and Colin

Acknowledgements

I wish to thank my family for their continued support in my need to put my stories into print. I would also like to thank those who have assisted in getting those stories out for others to read: Final Editor, Melanie Wilken; Editor, Jim Martyka; Iowa Editor, Kathy Shields; Production, Robin Thomas; Readers: Moni Richie, Steven Shibuya, Laurie Stevens and Nancy Cole Silverman.

GATEWAY TO EAGLES PARK

1982

Eagles Park is west of Pinkerton, Iowa on Highway 99, a road of S-curves, small dips and the route to the third and most popular tavern in the Pinkerton area; ED'S HOOF AND BEER. The park was once the home for Indians who used to bury their dead here because they claimed the land was sacred ground. For me, Eagles Park was a great place to find arrowheads if I looked hard enough.

Max Lamott said eagles flew in the park and the place was magical. He was an eighth Lakota on his father's mother's side. A taxidermist by trade, he spent most of his time sitting outside ED's asking for spare change or sipping a bottle of Thunderbird out of a brown paper sack.

You couldn't miss seeing him. His face reminded me of a cumulus cloud with his dark eyes jumping around as if worried he was going to miss out on something. Several tattoos marked his forehead. The markings weren't easy to make out from the deep wrinkles caused by his living mostly outside. The middle one etched black came across as an eagle, wings spread. From there, symbols marked his kin, maybe explaining the eagle. Strikes like lightning. Circles. They all reminded me of the hieroglyphs found on Egyptian pyramids in the *National Geographic*.

He always wore a leather vest, summer or winter, Indian-like, and a dark blue baseball hat with the word "Yankees" in large, white letters. He said the cap was a gift from someone who visited New York and threw it in the garbage when they got back home.

Max liked it when young people strayed from their parent's hands and came down to where he sat. The young stuck around to hear his stories. Like me. I couldn't get enough, and I didn't mind when he told me a story I'd heard before. They never were exactly the same.

There was one I wish I would have listened to a little closer. This story started with a young Indian girl walking down to the lake before the area was called Eagles Park. Max said she came to smell the flowers and wash off the long winter.

"This here brave from another tribe was in the woods that same day. Maybe he came thinking like she had. Or maybe he wandered out of the woods and crossed tribal boundary lines to poach himself some deer. I ain't sure. I don't reckon it matters why."

Max took a sip from his brown paper sack, his Adam's apple bobbing down a big gulp. His hair strayed wild both on his head and beard. His mouth and lips colored black. I remember being with my grandmother Gray once and us seeing him walking along the road. I told her how Max was an eighth Indian. She said Max Lamott was nothing but a Norwegian drunk and only a fool would listen to his nonsense.

"Boys liked to look at girls back then, too." Max slapped his knee seeing my face grow red. As red as my hair, I bet. "Come on now, boy," he guffawed. "What red-blooded man wouldn't take a peek around the bushes? You tellin' me you've never taken a gander at your sisters?" He slapped his knee again.

I burned.

He went on after a couple more swigs saying that when the Indian girl came out of the lake to dry herself, the brave came out of the bushes. "He grabbed her and did her wrong." He steadied me with a bird's eye. "You know what I mean by doing her wrong?"

My hair was probably a tame color now compared to my face.

I nodded. I had a vague notion.

He changed from the story. "What do you want to be when you grow up, boy?"

I needed no time to think. "A hero."

He took a drink and swished it around in his mouth. "Hero?" He swallowed, then spit. "I wanted to be a hero when I was a boy, but life didn't see it that way. The plan for me was to stumble until I fell and then sit here and wait to die." He leaned towards me. "You got the eyes, you know that boy? The pure type, I mean."

My mother called my eyes a rich hazel color, which was different from most people with red hair who had green eyes. Or blue, like most of my family. My dad said they were gold, not hazel, and that they were as unique as I was. My sister Shilo just said my eyes illustrated my deviant personality.

"You just might be a hero."

The comment made me feel older, wise. Heroic.

Max Lamott took a swig. His eyes bloodshot and yellow. "You listen careful, you hear me?"

He waited for me to nod.

"You listenin????"

I nodded again, big time.

"Evil begets evil. No getting away from it. No matter how hard you run." He took another sip and stared at his bottle a while. "I don't reckon I know how long I have. Days? Months? Years? Hell, I might not see the end of this here bottle. None of us knows. So I might as well give you one more piece of advice." He waited again, and I nodded again. "The real truth is that it doesn't matter if you get away or not. When they come after you, I mean. They come, you got to go."

I nodded but wasn't sure I understood.

"Not everything you don't understand in this life is evil. It just is."

He held up his bottle in its sack and hefted it, as if by its weight he could discern how many sips he had left. He licked his blackened lips with his brown stained tongue. And smiled, his teeth stained yellow from cheap tobacco and chew. "You got any money, boy?"

I shook my head.

He turned his head sideways, giving me a look from one eye, again a bird's eye watching a bug crawling in the grass. I was sure he was eyeing me again to see if I was telling the truth or not. He made as if to stand and staggered a step toward me. "Guess I'll be going, then." Quickly I reached in and pulled out the change in my pocket. He reached out, his broken nails raking the skin of my palm, slipping the quarters out and into his pocket with me hardly seeing his hand move.

He sat back down. "Now where was I? Yep, I remember. This Indian girl looked up into the clouds to thank the Great Spirit for giving her such a grand day to die on, and it was then she saw an eagle soar overhead. He was flying so high, it was as if he was flying in the heavens. Thinking the Great Spirit came to witness her death, she sang her praise from the depth of her heart. The eagle saw what was going on and heard her song. The eagle cawed and eight more eagles came. They all soared down to the earth to the water's edge. The main eagle picked up the girl and soared off into the clouds. The others stayed, plucked out the brave's eyes with their giant beaks, and ripped his heart out with their talons."

I gulped, imagining such a thing happening.

He took another long swallow from his paper bag. "Storytelling gives a man a thirst."

I asked him where the eagles took the girl but he said that wasn't part of the story. "Not this story anyway." As more questions came to me, I guess he thought it was best for the two of us to part ways. He took his empty bottle and my change and went into ED'S.

I never saw Max without a brown paper sack in his hand. Word on him was that he chewed a lot of peyote during what he called his cleansing period, which seemed to be a couple times a month. When I got older, I still stopped to hear his stories, although I didn't put as much stock in them as I had when I was young. But I wasn't the only kid who strayed to Max. He'd seeded his stories into other young minds.

Older, these kids joined me and Max in saying there was something different about Eagles Park. The word magical turned to haunted. A few swore they'd seen the ghost of the Indian girl alone in the moonlight bathing in the lake. There were even those who claimed to see the Indian brave, blood pouring out of his chest, his hands trying to hold his life back from draining out.

Very few today go into the park beyond the camping grounds after dark.

Max Lamott was a storyteller when I was a kid. He became a legend after he died.

He was said to have drowned in Eagles Lake. An empty bottle of Thunderbird and his baseball cap were found on the boat dock.

It was seven years after his death that things started happening in and around Pinkerton. The first thing to happen was Royce Martin. He came back from Eagles Park before his fishing line had a chance to get wet in the lake. He came back home and died.

CHAPTER ONE

1989

My name is Jakob Cahill but everyone calls me Jake.

I was fifteen years old and sitting in Clyde Buck's barbershop waiting my turn in the chair when Sheriff Boggs came in. Boggs stood well over six-foot-six in his stocking feet and was wide at the shoulders and chest. His family was known as Iowa-Russian on his mother's side, and his father's side said to be Iowa-German. He carried a five o'clock shadow even after he was freshly shaved. He had piercing, crystal-clear, blue eyes.

Sheriff Boggs didn't grab up the *Des Moines Chronicle* and sit down and wait his turn like I expected. Instead, he stood in the middle of the room, hands on his hips, rocking back and forth on his heels. A cigarette cupped in his palm curled up smoke.

Palmer Dodd sat in the chair talking to Buck and the rest of us about his sister's gallbladder operation. Sheriff Boggs interrupted and asked if any of us had seen Denver Wilcox around town that morning.

Officer Wilcox was one of Bogg's men. We all shook our heads.

He took a last hit off his cigarette and smashed it out in the ashtray. The telephone rang. The caller must have asked if the Sheriff was there, because Buck held out the phone. "It's Dr. Potter, Sheriff."

We all stayed quiet and listened to the Sheriff's side of the conversation. Royce Martin's name was mentioned. When the Sheriff hung up, Buck asked him if something was wrong but the Sheriff rushed out without answering, letting the door bang shut behind him. The lights on his car swirled and the siren wailed as he sped away.

"Wonder what's up?" Buck said.

The rest of us were wondering the same.

I sat in the chair when Stover Roe came into the shop. He panted, seeming a bit breathless. He asked the room if we all had heard the news.

"Heard we might be expecting some bad weather later on today," Buck offered.

"I'm not talking about a little rain, here." Stover's voice raised a notch. "My wife Eunice got a call from Helen Day. You know, the

Days live next door to the Royce Martin place. Something is going on out there."

Buck made a clip or two with his scissors and said, to show he was in the news loop, "Sheriff was just here. Dr. Potter called asking him to go out to the Martin's. Did Royce have an attack?"

Buck meant a heart attack. It was the number one killer of most men around sixty in Pinkerton at the time.

Stover shook his head. "Helen Day told Eunice that Ethel Martin screamed like the house was on fire. I guess Dalbert was sitting on the john and she said he jumped up, pulled on his pants, and ran straight on over. Helen said when he got over to the Martin's and saw Royce, he barely recognized him. His hair was pure white."

"Hair can turn with an attack. Hair's fragile." Buck remarked.

I didn't know the Martins well. Royce Martin owned the General Store. The store sold things people needed a little above prices they could afford until they got up to Des Moines to Walmart. However, I could pick Royce out on the street. Around the age of my grandparents, maybe seventy, eighty, he had this way of walking, like he was balancing on a ship. It was caused by his artificial hip making one of his legs slightly shorter than the other.

Buck stopped snipping at my head and told Stover Roe he'd better sit down or he was going to have an attack. Stover took a seat, his rotund body filling most of the chair so the rest of him hung out. He sat with his knees spread and his hands clasped between them.

After a couple of breaths and a wheeze, Stover said, "I just saw Royce early this morning with his fishing pole in hand. I'd swear he didn't look no different than he did when I saw him at church on Sunday. I'd swear to that." He waited for the rest of us to agree then that it must be true. Stover and Eunice weren't known to preach your ear off, but they were good Christians, never missed a Sunday at His Holy Word Calvary Church. "Dalbert must have thought Royce had an attack. He told Helen to call the paramedics. She said she already had. He said then he wasn't sure what to do next. You know, if he should give Royce artificial respiration or pump his chest."

He took in a deep breath and exhaled, letting his body shake off his nerves. "According to Helen Day, Ethel told Dalbert she was surprised to find Royce back home so soon from fishing. He hadn't been gone that long. She'd been in the kitchen, having done up the breakfast dishes and thinking about doing a load of wash when she saw Royce standin' in the doorway. He was holding his chest and lookin' outside. Then he turned and tried to tell her something. I guess she couldn't understand a word he was sayin'."

Buck interrupted. "Sounds like an attack. My brother's wife said he was standing in their bedroom holding onto his chest like that when he had his."

Stover went on. "Well, Ethel went up to him to see if he was okay. And when she got his attention, he fell down right at her feet. She screamed to beat hell."

18

I listened as Buck asked Stover to tell it all again, and the two of them tried to figure out if Royce had a stroke or heart attack. They each had their opinion and their other relatives' tragedies to back up their theories.

When Buck took off the cape and brushed off the back of my neck, I glanced in the mirror. My hair definitely was short, way shorter than I'd asked to have it, and I knew it was going to get me some heckling once school started. The shape appeared a bit uneven on one side. But I knew it would be useless to complain. The haircut was as good as I was going to get with Stover in the shop spilling the news he'd brought with him to tell.

Everyone was talking about Royce Martin that day. Either him or the storm expected sometime in the evening. Storms had been traveling around us a lot--north, south, east. One slipped by without hitting us. It skimmed across the open fields a mile away to the west. If it had hit Pinkerton, there would have been hell to pay. A funnel did hit and tore up Corpus, a small, nearby town, ripping apart the high school and causing several people to get hurt.

My friends and I sat and watched that storm from the roof of my house. You couldn't see the town, but you could watch the lightning strikes. Like most storms, it was clear before gray, loose clouds marched past with a black, heavy mass following, booming low, weighted cannon blasts. The drumming booms rolling across the low, open land made me think how us sitting there eating and

But Lilly got ahead of her, adding, "What good was it to try to bring him back to life? It sounds to me like he was dead by the time the doctor got there."

The two women gave Lilly's opinion some consideration. Then Lilly said, as if she'd been there to watch it all, "The doctor listened to Royce's heart. He said Royce was dead. But when Dr. Potter got out one of those little flashlights of his and shined the light into Royce's eyes, Royce suddenly reached up."

Kate gasped holding onto her heart. She stared with disbelief.

The waitress about dropped the coffee cup she was filling.

My mouth hung open. It was a shock. Like one of those Alfred Hitchcock movies.

Lilly nodded her head letting Kate know she was telling her the truth. "Helen said Dalbert told her it about scared him to death."

"Would me, too," Kate finally got to comment.

"Royce grabbed Dr. Potter's stethoscope, almost choked Dr. Potter to death, and Royce tried to tell him somethin'. Helen said Dalbert only caught one word."

What was it? It was the same question I was asking. But I am sure the waitress and Kate wondered the same.

Lilly shrugged. "I didn't ask. What's it matter? Royce passed on."

It was killing me. What one word did Royce say with his last breath of life?

Lilly and Kate exchanged expressions of meaningful sympathy. The waitress left her eavesdropping to interrupt mine. "What will it be today, Jake? Cheeseburger or Maid-Rite?"

I ordered a cheeseburger with everything. The waitress left to put in the order and get my Coke. When I glanced back to the booth, I found Lilly and Kate leaving. As they passed behind me, Lilly said, "But that's not everything going on around here. You heard, didn't you? Someone found Denver Wilcox's patrol car at Eagles Lake."

When the waitress came back with my Coke, I asked her if she'd heard anything about Officer Wilcox. She said she hadn't heard a word. So I shared how Sheriff Boggs came into Buck's barbershop looking for him when the call came in about Royce Martin.

"He was dead?"

"That's what I heard. But don't know from what."

"It's this heat," she said, wiping her forehead with the back of her hand. Then she said how it was just going on noon and the lunch crowd would bring in more news.

By the time I was done with my cheeseburger, the Owl was full of people talking about both Royce Martin and Officer Wilcox. They seemed to be comparing the facts of what they heard and from who to whom. I caught snatches here and there. What I learned was pretty much what I'd already heard or guessed. Both men were dead.

After lunch, I headed for home. That's when I saw Teddy Templeton sitting on the cannon in front of Pinkerton City Hall. He was wearing a red-billed cap marked in white block letters, "Cardinals."

CHAPTER TWO

The Pitts family lived about a mile away from our house. I was sweatin' like a turkey at Thanksgiving by the time I got there. When Mrs. Pitts saw me, she went to the refrigerator and got me a cold pop. It tasted good rushing down my throat.

I found Pitts in his room working a Rubik's Cube. Oliver Shelden Pitts was his name, but we called him Pitts. He might be called a hoarder. He's the type who couldn't throw anything away. The floor in his room was heaped with cubing magazines, car auction newspapers, every assignment ever done since the first grade, plastic bags and bottles, balls of string, rubber bands, boxes of tacks, arrowheads, rocks he'd found and liked, rocks he didn't like and set aside to throw away, piles of clothes, old slices of pizza and stale, uneaten sandwiches on plates. Sometimes it was hard to see the carpet when you came into his room. But he was pretty good at

25

keeping somewhat organized. At least he kept direct paths to his desk, chairs, bed and closet, where more of his clothes lay piled in a heap.

He dressed like a hoarder, too. Even though it was hot enough outside to fry an egg and hot enough in his room to melt the butter to fry it in, he was wearing three tank tops (red, blue and green), old jeans cut ragged into shorts and black socks with flip flops. His green tank had large white letters that read "NEVER FORGET" above the photo of a dodo bird.

Pitts was a bit eccentric and a sore spot to his mother's housekeeping, and he was the smartest guy in our freshman class. Teachers said he would have his pick at colleges--UI, MIT or Harvard. But when asked, he'd say he wasn't sure if he was even going to college, stating he thought established education limited learning.

He cubed whenever he had something serious to think about. So immediately, I guessed he'd heard what was going on in town.

"Hey, who butchered you?" Walter Bryan Forester, sitting in a chair close to a large pile of magazines with a couple cubing ones on top, appeared to have given up playing his Gameboy to check out the latest *Playboy*. He looked over as I came in. I went over and ripped the issue out of his hands. He'd been looking at the centerfold, and I let it hang open taking a good gander myself.

Pitts' older brother Jimmy was a student at UI. He'd been home all summer giving us a full library including_*Penthouse*, *Juggs* and my personal favorite, *Hustler.*

"Hey, give it back," he yelled, reaching up to snatch it out of my hands.

We called Walter, Diddleman. He was short with kind of a square head, light blue eyes, and bad acne. He was stocky but more muscular than fat, and he wrestled on the high school team. You might think that'd give him an edge with the jocks, but wrestling wasn't considered a jock sport. Not at Pinkerton anyway. In fact, most jocks thought wrestling pretty gay for guys; wearing tight leotards, grabbing the butts of other sweaty, slippery guys.

Being a jock meant you played on the football or baseball team. Cheerleaders hung on your muscles. He was called Diddleman because his hands were always in his pockets.

"Why don't you read something good?" I flipped pages.

"Like what?"

I'd just finished reading Dante's *Inferno*. Mr. Danvers, my English teacher, saw me reading H. P. Lovecraft's *Cthulhu Mythos* and he offered me a list of other work he thought I might like: Poe, Shelly, Stevenson, Stoker. I'd seen most of the movies but I'd never read the books. When I picked up Dante's *Inferno,* I thought Mr. Danvers was playing with me. Thinking he'd get me to read *real literature*, as he called it, instead of reading science fiction or horror.

The whole book is one long poem. Poetry wasn't my game. But figuring he'd asked me if I read it, I picked it up. I got hooked right away.

I knew there was no reasoning with Diddleman on how the ginormous rush from walking through the horrors of Hell could match the pleasure of playing with big boobs.

"Here." I handed it back. "I've seen better."

"Yeah? Where? Oh, let me guess, Ammmmy." He hung his tongue out of his mouth like a dog panting and started pounding his fist on his leg. "Oh, Amy. Stop. No...don't...stop."

"Quit being a jerk." I threw a punch at his arm, but he saw it coming and leaned over. I didn't cut back fast enough. My hand hit the back of his chair, popping my knuckles.

I shook the pain off as Diddleman got up, moving away from me while throwing boxer punches. "Don't mess with the man."

Moving over to the bed, I threw a pile of clothes off onto the floor.

"Hey, quit messing up my room," Pitts yelled.

The truth needs to be said sometimes. "Your room's already a mess."

The bed smelled rank, a combination of summer sweat and yanking off, like the sheets hadn't been washed for a long time. I crossed my ankles and cupped the back of my head in my fingers.

"Royce Martin fell over dead this morning." I said it plain and simple like that. "He said only one word before he died."

"Shit?" Diddleman exclaimed.

We ignored him. Pitts asked, "What was it?"

"Lilly March didn't ask."

"Really?" Pitts grunted. "I read an article that stated women have four times the curiosity of men." He paused, thoughtful. "Last word, huh? A last word should be something revealing."

Pitts' black hair was cut high over his ears and the front fell down into his eyes behind thick-framed, black glasses. His glasses had slipped down his nose.

"Maybe it was Eagles," I suggested. "He'd been fishing over at Eagles Park." Or maybe his wife's name, Ethel.

Pitts continued to cube, then said, as matter-of-factly, "Officer Wilcox was found dead, too."

I wasn't surprised Pitts knew about Royce and Wilcox. In Pinkerton, you don't always need to move around to hear the latest. Bad news finds you.

"Any thoughts?" Again, I'd figured that's why he was cubing.

"Can't speculate." He stopped his fingers, thinking, his forehead wrinkling. He stared over at the wall as if there was something there for him to study. Only, there wasn't anything but a *Hannibal* movie poster next to posters of *Alien I*, *Alien II* and *Alien III*, and posters of

OUTRÉ

old rock groups, The Grateful Dead and The Rolling Stones. His walls matched the room's decor.

He pushed his glasses back on the bridge of his nose and began chewing on the inside of his cheek like he always did when something was puzzling him. My mom said the poor boy was going to chew a hole right through if he didn't stop.

He hedged. "Besides, I don't want to say anything until the storm's passed."

"Storm? What's the storm got to do with anything?" It was damn hot in the room and dark clouds had been moving towards Pinkerton most of the day. "They say it probably'll go south and not hit us."

Pitts went back to cubing, but he must have been trying some of his blindfolding techniques this time because his eyes were half closed, eyelashes fluttering, not paying attention to the cube as he twisted white cubes one way, red cubes the other, blue this way, red back. He'd played in a couple of cube contests.

"Did you hear Royce Martin lost a lot of blood but no puncture wounds?"

I hadn't, but waited. I figured he had more.

"Officer Wilcox was found with a puncture wound in his chest."

"How'd you hear all this?"

He opened his eyes and gave me a *Duh!* expression. Of course, his mom was a nurse at Pinkerton General Hospital. He could have gotten some of the cause of death news from her.

I asked, "How could Royce lose blood without puncture wounds?"

"Vampires," Diddleman answered, holding the magazine again. It fell as he straightened his arms in front of him like a Frankenstein monster and stomped over toward me on the pathway from the chair to the bed. "I vant to drink vour bloooood."

"Quit being a choad, Diddleman. Frankenstein wasn't a vampire. Besides, this is serious business."

I pushed Diddleman away. He stumbled back, knocking things over.

Pitts put his cube down on a cardboard table piled with writing pads, books, half empty glasses of clotted milk and a test tube filled with something green and fuzzy. He took a small scratch piece of paper from off the table. It was bleeding with ink, but he checked his watch and noted the time on it. Then he got up and went over to his desk.

It, too, was a hazard of stacks. He pulled out from under one stack a drawing book. He located a half-chewed-pencil, its eraser twisted into a scrap of metal, and came back to his chair. Putting his socked, flip-flop foot across a leg sprouting thick black hairs, he opened the tablet and started flipping some pages.

We were all familiar with what was in the book. Or at least Pitts and I were. "None of them talk about people found dead or finding any description like Royce Martin's."

He kept searching, reading. Flipping one page for another. Looking at one pasted photo then the next. The book was a collection of alien sightings. He was far more obsessed than I was on UFOs. He surfed the Web for hours looking for information.

"Hey, come on you guys," Diddleman cried. "Aliens wouldn't come to Pinkertown. Most of us want out."

Diddleman had a good point.

"Who said they'd be coming specifically to Pinkerton?" Pitts paused. "But then, why not Pinkerton? No one would notice them in Hollywood. Or New York. It's people who live in places like ours that spot these types of unidentified objects. The world's got to wake up. They exist."

Diddleman wasn't buying it. "How do you know?"

"I ask questions and read, you choad. You might want to pick up a book."

Both Pitts and I had both read with enthusiasm Erich von Däinken's *Chariots of the Gods*. I backed Pitts. "There are archaeological sites showing evidence of possible spacemen, and I read where sightings have been recorded since the written word"

Diddleman flipped Pitts and me off and went back to his Playboy. "Don't believe it. Nothing about them in the Bible."

Pitts looked miffed. Sometimes he didn't have patience for Diddleman's lack of curiosity. He lowered the book. "Okay, let's put it in your terms."

Diddleman sat back down in his chair. Maybe he was curious just what kind of terms he might have.

"You believe in sex, right?'

Diddleman's curiosity shot up. "You're talkin' to the man."

"Sex, meaning two people, not just you and your hand. You gettin' any?"

By the finger he gave Pitts, Diddleman wasn't happy with the slant this discussion was now taking.

Pitts continued. "But you believe there's sex between a man and a woman, right? Yet, you haven't seen or done shit. Which means you believe sex is real although you have never observed it."

This time Diddleman's finger raised higher with a hard thrust. He got up, bypassing the selected routes through the room and knocking more things over in his hurry.

"A little hard on him, don't you think?" I asked once Diddleman's over-the-top exit was finished.

Pitts shrugged. "Yeah, maybe. But sometimes I can't figure out why I'm friends with the guy. He doesn't hold more than one thought in his head at a time."

"Ah, let's see? Could it be because we've been friends since grade school? And that he'd walk the desert without a drop of water if either one of us asked him to? You know Diddleman has our backs like we have his."

Pitts didn't say anything in return, but he couldn't do anything else but agree. We'd all known each other that long.

Pitts and I both were raised in fairly normal homes. I'm talking about us both having a mom and a dad that gave a damn about us. Diddleman's dad drank his breakfast and his mom gave most of her money to the church, praying for a miracle she'd wake up to the life as she dreamed it.

"You know we are about all the family he has that really gives a damn about him."

"His folks give a damn," Pitts fired back.

"Maybe." I went over and recovered the Gameboy and put the video device in the chair knowing Diddleman would be back. None of us stayed mad very long. I was off the selected room routes now, too. Moving around to pick up other things that had fallen. But when I'd pick something up to put it back in place, I'd knock something else over.

"Hey man, leave my stuff alone. I have this room organized." Pitts shut the book. "Okay, I'll go find him and tell him what an asshole I can be. In case he forgot." He tossed the book to me.

"I think sorry's enough." I grinned and held up the book. "What do you want me to do with this?"

"Start looking through the articles and confirm what I've already found.

"What'd you find?"

"Not saying yet. See if you can find any similarities. When did the sightings occur? What was happening at the same time? What happened after? That kind of thing."

After he left the room, I began flipping pages, scanning clippings and articles, photos and glancing at Pitts' notes and underlines. We'd gathered a lot of articles on Roswell. Other pages held newspaper clippings reporting sporadic UFO sightings. More states than Nevada had reported seeing strange things in the sky. Seldom was the word "alien" used. Most of the time anything unexplained was called "unidentified flying object."

I'd asked Pitts once, "What do the aliens say when they see our satellites and rockets? Do they call our stuff UFOs?"

He busted a gut. "They call them EFOs: Earthling's Flying Objects. You can be sure they know who we are and what we're doing." When he finished guffawing at his own joke, he began speaking about the Big Bang. Pitts could actually read a science book and understand what it said.

"They're way ahead of our future."

He tried explaining the theory to me, but I was, and still am, more of a storyteller than a scientist. When I reminded Pitts, he said I'd eventually see how to combine the two, writers like Isaac Asimov,

Arthur C. Clark, Ray Bradbury or Paul Scanlon. Pitts had read most of my stories and said I had a knack for creating pictures with words.

Alone in the room, I started getting sleepy and desperate for air. It wasn't just hot, it'd turned muggy. A stream dribbled from my pits to the waistband of my shorts. Getting up, I licked the salt off my sweat mustache and swiped at the watershed forming under my hairline.

Pressure, too, was forming above my eyes, like a headache starting to build. My dad said I inherited his headaches and it was something I was going to have to learn to live with. Most weren't as bad as the ones he'd get, yet he said his got worse as he got older.

I opened a window and a breeze came through, drying some of the sweat off my face, but it began causing havoc in the room. Loose papers took flight along with dust mites. I closed it. If Pitts got pissed with me for cleaning up the stuff Diddleman knocked over, he might get madder than hell letting his dust mites out of their cages.

It was when I was closing the window that I saw the sky was getting darker, and I thought maybe the weatherman had gotten it wrong. From where I was standing, it looked like the storm had turned and was heading straight toward Pinkerton.

Pitts and Diddleman returned, laughing like there had never been a problem. They were drinking Cokes and I grabbed one. Nothing better on a hot, sweltering day than an icy, cold Coke rushing down your throat. It's the real thing.

Pitts went back to cubing. Diddleman picked up the Gameboy and re-sat his butt in the chair. I'd given the book what I thought was a close scrutiny replaced it on the desk informing Pitts I didn't find anything. At least, I didn't see anything like what he'd been talking about.

He got up, came over, took it back over to the chair next to him. Looking as if he hardly missed a beat on the cube, his fingers returned to rotating the cubes in a rhythmic rhythm. *Turn, twist, turn, turn, twist.* "It might be a stretch," he finally said, glancing over at Diddleman, "but, I'm still saying it's possible."

Diddleman stopped gaming. "What, me getting laid?

I didn't want to go down that bumpy road, so I asked, "What'd you find?"

"Like I said, I don't want to speculate. I need to get more intel."

CHAPTER THREE

Dark clouds marched over Pinkerton. I biked home without making another stop. Mom was just coming out the back door with her hands full. "Good, Jake. You're home. Help me with these things."

My mom was a Tupperware junkie. Our kitchen cupboards were full of snap-on containers, bowls or lettuce keepers…yes, we had more than one lettuce keeper. And we didn't eat that much lettuce. In her arms were a Tupperware cake carrier, casserole keeper, storage container full of cookies and a bowl of what looked like pasta salad. I took a few of the containers out of her arms and began to unseal the cookie container.

Chewbacca, our over-weight, chocolate Labrador, followed her out. He kept a good eye on most of us, but with mom, it's like dad said, he wasn't stupid. He kept to her like gum on a shoe knowing who poured the kibble. Spotting me pulling out a cookie, he came up to me into his best sit position, tail *thump, thump, thumping.* Mom noticed. "Jake, get out of those. I'm taking them over to the Martin's and the Wilcox family."

At the first word of tragedy, especially when it came to death in a family, the women of the Pinkerton Lady's Club turned on their ovens. Grief here spurred appetites.

Her reprimand to stay out came after I'd already snagged a Snickerdoodle, so I figured I couldn't put it back. I mean, I could have germs. So I popped it in my mouth, chewing when she wasn't looking. Chewbacca still mirrored my every move, checking the ground for crumbs. *Sorry,* I mouthed.

We got the containers in the trunk, and I went to head back in to the kitchen to see if she'd made a double batch and left some cookies for the rest of us, but she said, "Come with me. I'll need help. Besides, I want to get there and back before it begins to storm."

I shrugged and again mouthed *"Sorry"* to a still awaiting Chewbacca, whispering I'd make it up to him when I got back. He then followed me over to the car thinking I was going to open the back door for him, but mom said he wasn't going. A huge disappointment. But both he and I knew there was no use to argue.

We went to the Martins' place first. They lived across town over by the Hy-Vee grocery on the way to Highway 99. Cars were parked in the driveway and along the road.

You could smell the Martin place before you rounded the corner and got there. The Martins were hog farmers. Nothing smellier than hog crap on a hot day.

Mom picked up the pasta salad bowl and cookie container. "Stay here, I'll be right back." Apparently I wasn't needed. Maybe she just wanted the company for the drive. I popped the door open to give myself some air. It didn't help with the heat or the stench. I got out.

Breathing through my mouth, I took a walk over and around to the barn and hog lot. Even the hogs seemed too weak to move. A cloud of flies buzzed on and off their pale, fat bodies with barely an ear twitching.

On my arrival, the flies smelled fresh meat and came looking for me. I turned around to head the heck out of there, swatting a cloud of them off me, when my eyes took in the fenced pasture about a hundred yards away. I noticed a heap of brown and realized the shape was a cow lying on its side. Unusual. On a whole, cows generally stay in a herd. Even a cow has the good sense to get downwind of a pen of hogs.

Cows get down on their bellies by pulling their legs in under them and hang their heads while they sleep. It also wasn't unheard of for them to lie on their sides. So I figured, on a hot day like today, who didn't want a nap? Still swatting off black, stinging bites, I felt moved to check it out.

Coming up closer, a huge cloud of flies buzzed. Heat seems to inspire flies. Then *it* hit me. Pig crap was a flowery bouquet compared to the putrid stink coming off this cow. I inched up closer and stretched my neck to see. I gagged at the sight of dried blood, chips of bone and a dark, black-cherry red hole in the middle of its forehead. It was as if someone had taken a sledgehammer, punched a hole in its head and then ripped its brain out. And I saw something else, lying off about another fifty yards. Another cow? No, smaller. A hog?

"Jake, let's go."

I ran back to the car. "Someone killed one of the Martin's cows." I pointed toward the fence, although nothing could be seen from this viewpoint.

Her eyes followed to where I pointed but she was more concerned about making her next stop. "Nobody killed it, Jake. It probably died. Besides, it's the least of the Martin's problems, right now." She got into the car saying, "Get in. It's beginning to rain."

I felt a drop and noticed how the wind picked up. I got in the car telling her what I saw. She ended up agreeing it was peculiar, but, "There's probably a good reason. Maybe Royce put it down and didn't get around to taking care of it." I told her about how it looked like its brain had been ripped out of its head, and then about how I'd seen something else, maybe one of the hogs dragged into the pasture. Again, she shrugged off the two incidents.

My mom had little imagination. Everything, she claimed, had a good reason. Except, of course, when Shilo or I did something she didn't approve of. Then there was no reasoning for it.

The Wilcox family lived down the street from the Baptist Church. The church parking lot full, and it wasn't even Wednesday night Bible Study.

The wind had picked up. Rain plopped on the windshield. A blast of thunder warned from a distance. Reverend Hunsicker came out of the church walking beside a woman, her shoulders slouched with the burden she was carrying. He had an arm around her and held his other hand above her head as if to shelter her from more trouble befalling her. They both walked in the direction of the Wilcox house.

Mom gave me the same instructions as last time, emphasizing this time for me to stay put. She'd only be a minute. But again, her minute could turn out to be an hour. I figured she'd be gone at least ten or fifteen, so I got out, staying close, and checked around. I spotted a Pinkerton city police car over in the church lot and recognized the officer leaning against it. I'd be able to keep an eye on the Wilcox door and the car from there, so I moseyed over to see what I could work out of him about what had happened to Officer Wilcox.

Pinkerton's city police department was pretty small. It was a small town. There wasn't much crime other than drinking and drugs, speeding and underage sex. Sometimes in that same order. The city police handled the mayhem within the city limits. The County Sheriff's department handled all of Circlegold County, including the parks if the State Police or rangers weren't available.

"Hey, Officer Hayworth." Most of we kids knew Officer Hayworth. He visited the middle school and high school yearly to give an assembly on "Just say no to drugs."

He gave a nod acknowledging my approach. "Jake Cahill. Do I have the name right?"

"You do." I'd interviewed him for the *Prowler*, our school newspaper. I performed a customary notice to the menacing clouds hovering out on the horizon. "Looks like a storm's coming," I said.

"Looks like it's already here." He put his palm out as if to catch raindrops.

"If this is all we're goin' to get," I put my hand out as well, "we won't get enough to water the lawn." My hand came back dry.

"Saves you from having to mow it," he said with an air of authority.

He had a small swell in his lower lip where he'd tucked some Skoal chewing tobacco to enjoy while he kept the peace during the unscheduled gathering. He was so skinny his hipbones barely held up his duty belt and gun, the reason he was continually readjusting them. It gave his manner a more nervous and fidgety appearance. He reminded me a little of Barney Fife on old The Andy Griffith Show reruns.

"Crazy what happened to Officer Wilcox."

He turned his head to the side away from the both of us and spit yellow into the grass. His attention went back to those exiting the church.

I tried again, "Story's all over town with two different theories. One says Officer Wilcox had a heart attack, like Royce Martin. The other says he'd been shot."

"Wasn't shot." He spit again, tonguing his chew back into place. He hefted his gun belt. "Once we find who did this, there's going to be hell to pay."

"You think someone did this? Are you saying someone killed Officer Wilcox and Royce Martin?"

He spit again, the juice really flowing now. "You just never mind. You let the police handle things." Again his belt slipped as it did each time he went to spit, sucking in enough breath to get well past any walking area, his gun belt slid toward his knees.

"Remember this, Cahill." He put his hand onto the gun's holster as if getting ready should the murderer run out of the church or down the street at the same moment we were discussing him. "When a crime's done to one of us," he pointed to his badge, "the act's done to us all. No sir, we won't rest until it's been solved."

Curious, since while the city police and county operated to keep citizens and communities safe, most in Pinkerton knew there was a huge dislike between Chief Moore and Sheriff Boggs. Not that they didn't officially work together. I think it was a personal dislike. My dad said Sheriff Boggs wouldn't walk on the same side of the street as Purvis Moore.

He spit, hefted, "We'll get this here all sewed up by nightfall."

He gave another couple of spits and tugs then turned and got in his car. As soon as he was settled, he picked up his radio mic. I couldn't hear what he said but heard a voice on the radio say something back about Eagles Park. He started the motor then rolled down the window. "You hear anything, Cahill, you bring it straight to me. You hear? Don't be passing it around. Things like this get people stirred up."

"Sure will." I was just about to confirm he might be heading out to Eagles Park, when I heard, "Jake! I thought I told you to stay in the car."

Officer Hayworth raised the window and drove on. I ran over and jumped into our car.

"It was too hot in the car," I explained.

She dabbed her forehead with a Kleenex. "It's going to storm good. And at a time like this." She was big on pointing out how the weather never matched the social event. It wasn't proper for it to storm when people were grieving. Or to rain at someone's wedding.

Wind ruined birthday picnic parties. And a hot sunny day was never acceptable when there was too much to do.

The rain held to its slow *drip-drop* on the windshield. Mom started wondering aloud if maybe she needed to cook up more food. "There're so many people coming in and out, what's there will go fast." While she considered whether to bake a pie and another casserole, my thoughts drifted to Officer Hayworth. Were Officer Wilcox and Royce Martin killed? How?

Both mom and I pulled up short seeing Teddy Templeton riding his bike along the road, heading in the direction we were coming from. He had on his Cardinals cap with his head butting against the sprinkling.

"Where's that boy going?" She slowed the car. "He'll be drenched. I bet Tira doesn't know he's out riding around in this weather."

Tira Templeton was Teddy's mother. It was the general consensus of folks that she tried to keep tabs on Teddy, but it always seemed like she was out searching for him. He wasn't hyper-active or rebellious. He was just...well, Teddy. He couldn't be pigeon-holed to a type.

Believe me, some have tried. First, specialists said she needed to put him in a special needs school, only to find he wasn't mentally challenged. In fact, when tested, they'd found Teddy was some sort of genius.

He suffered physically. His arms were longer than most people's and his eyes appeared lidless. He barely had any hair on his legs, chest or head. Almost bald at seventeen made him really stand out. He was a freshman like me but older because he got so lost in the "what to do with him" system.

But it was his behavior that bothered people the most. He didn't talk much. He'd stealthily come up next to someone without them knowing and creep them out. Plus his index finger, his pickin' finger, was longer than his middle finger. With it, he had a nasty habit of scrutinizing what came out of his nose and ears with that finger, and tasting it. A real turn off.

Most of the time, I felt sorry for him. It's hard enough to be a kid, let alone be a strange kid. Pitts once diagnosed him with a couple of possible diseases he'd researched on Yahoo, but Diddleman, like others, thought the guy was *wacko*.

We pulled into the drive at our place to find Chewbacca with company. Pitts and Diddleman were sitting on the porch. Chewbacca gave a bark and lolloped out to meet the car. When we got out, I gave him a good rubdown, while mom walked over asking what Pitts and Diddleman were doing gallivanting around when a storm was forecasted. Pitts told her the worst of the storm was heading south.

"See," he said, "it stopped raining."

Dark clouds still loomed overhead with heavy bellies and they were moving fast across the sky, but he was right, the rain had stopped. Darker clouds, so dark they appeared burnt green, stuck stalled to the horizon.

Mom said she would check the news channel herself and then proclaimed she was going in to make our dinner. She told Diddleman and Pitts they were invited to stay. Diddleman liked the idea, but Pitts said his mom invited us to his house, if that was all right with her.

He said, "Mr. Hamilton gave us a science project last year. We're supposed to have it ready by the beginning of school. That's in two weeks."

Mom paused, holding the door in her hand. Her head was cocked as if something didn't sound right. "You have an assignment for the first day of school?" She glanced over at me.

I had nothing, no idea what Pitts was talking about, and it was news to me I'd been invited over to his house for dinner.

"It's a science project," Diddleman seconded the fact with far too much enthusiasm. Diddleman avoided homework.

Mom gave each of us the same *something fishy is going on here* look. One of those stares that pierces through you as if she had the ability to read the guilt moving around in your conscious. "Well, I'd hate to have you start off high school on the wrong foot. But if that storm turns and begins to head this way, Jake, I want you back in the house where I know you're safe." She glanced out to the horizon, her eyes worrying.

"I'll be home early."

Her eyes came back to me. Unsure.

"Promise." I added.

She opened the door wider to slip inside, catching Chewbacca nudging his head though to go behind her. "Stay outside." His ears drooped and tail went limp.

"So, what's up?" I asked, curious about the deception.

Pitts headed over to where he and Diddleman had laid their bikes. Even then, he continued to watch the house, making sure the coast was clear before answering. Figuring mom was out of hearing distance, he pushed his glasses back up onto the bridge of his nose and said, "After you left, I cross-checked some of the things I'd found with some of the stuff we'd been collecting." He glanced over to Diddleman. "Give him the stuff."

Diddleman pulled an envelope out from his shirt and handed it over. Pitts removed some papers and thumbed through it. "Listen to this. Up by Spirit Lake a family was having a party in the middle of August when a storm came up. They claimed they saw something shiny come out of the clouds. It had a dome and a flat bottom. And there were red lights around it, but they didn't blink off and on. It wasn't a plane or anything. They said they watched it move from north to south."

He went to another page. "And then I found this other article where just days later there was a sighting in Spencer. Again, a storm came up out of nowhere, knocking the socks off the meteorologists, and a tornado touched down. The town was hardly touched, but two old guys were found dead and three girls came up missing. That was five years ago."

I went to interrupt him, but he held up a hand stopping me. "Two years after that, there were two sightings, one in Emmettsville. August, again. Again a bad storm. A person reported seeing something shaped like a triangle in the sky. He said it wasn't anything like he'd seen before. He said he went in the house to get his wife, wanting to show her, I guess, and when they both come out, there were more triangles. He said they watched the triangles and lights hover for a long while, red lights, but again none of them blinking, and then they just disappeared. Vanished so fast, he said, that by the time he blinked they were gone. When he called the police, he couldn't get through. The 911 number was busy. Meaning more people than him and his wife were witnesses."

I went to reach to read the pages myself. He pulled his hand and the papers back. "I'm not done. Far from it. In fact, I've saved the best for last. Cedar Falls. More than one person reported how it looked like a storm was coming their way, although the news hadn't announced any thunderstorms or tornado warnings. People started calling the police, talking about how something was appearing out of the clouds. A light, or what they said looked like a light, and there was something flying around. The police thought it was a hoax. Meth heads or something. Only a cop who didn't want his name used, he saw it, too. He said at first he thought he was seeing lightning but then things other than electricity started flying out of the clouds. Again, he said they looked like flying triangles."

"These stories could all be made up," I contended. "It's hot in August. People drink a lot of beer. Hell, I could use one."

"Hell, yeah. Me too," Diddleman croaked.

"I might agree with you both," Pitts acknowledged. "Only we have a cop recorded here as a witness. And there's more." He pulled more pages out. He held these up, as if offering undisputed proof. "This time no tornadoes touched down, but a man was reported killed." His eyes came off the pages and caught mine. "And a girl turned up missing."

"How old?" Diddleman wondered, as if this was the first he'd heard of it.

"What's that matter?" Pitts returned.

Diddleman shrugged. "Just asking."

"Are you seriously trying to say tell me the sightings and storms have something to do with what happened out at Eagles Park?"

His voice lowered to a tone which meant he was serious. "Look, Jake, it sounds crazy. But real always sounds crazy at first. I'm sure when people thought the world was flat and someone said its round, they thought it was the craziest thing they'd ever heard. People thought Galileo was crazy when he theorized the Earth moved around the sun. There are still people who argue the Holocaust never happened or landing on the moon was faked by the government."

"My dad said there was no way landing on the moon could be faked. Astronauts would never go along with it."

"He should know,' Pitts said, "working for NASA and all. Have you ever asked him about UFOs?"

"We've talked about it, but he said he'd never seen one."

"But I heard one of the astronauts said they did. Didn't he tell you about that?"

I shook my head. Dad wasn't much of a talker.

Pitts went back to his point. "I found these same type of similarities when looking through our book. When I asked you to look through it, I hoped you would confirm I wasn't just putting three plus two together to make four. Only, you weren't seeing what I was. So I started surfing after you left and found sightings like these in Marshalltown, Clear Lake, Knoxville, Storm Lake. It's like whatever is flying around out there is checking out the whole state. And get this, all the sightings reported happened in August. Storms occurred with each of them. And all were at places with bodies of water."

"What August doesn't have storms?" I retorted. I was just as fascinated as Pitts with what he'd found, but he and I had always sparred with each other as a means of coming to the right conclusion. I knew he didn't want me to just leap in and agree with him.

"Right. But then, I found this." He took one more sheet out of the envelope and held it up as if it were special. "This was reported in the Frytown Press just a month ago." It was a printed copy of a newspaper article. He turned it around as if offering for me to read it for myself. "Two girls came up missing." He let it fall to the ground. He pulled out and held out another printed article. "This was reported in Placerville. I almost missed it because it wasn't reported like a sighting. Two girls missing. They disappeared after a storm moved through the area." He let this one fall, too.

Frytown was three hours away, over by Iowa City area. However, Placerville was just a stone's throw away from Pinkerton.

I picked up both sheets off the ground and took the envelope out of his hand before he could toss the whole thing onto the ground. I was getting his point. He was damn serious.

He waited while I stood reading the thrown pages. Weathermen hadn't noticed any sudden barometric changes. Both events reported eyewitnesses saying how they saw something flying around out of the storm. The last one, in Placerville, reported a dark triangle-like object.

"There's more," Pitts said, his face reflecting the still skeptical question in my head. "I just ran out of paper to print. Cities around lakes like Spirit Lake, Okoboji, Dog Creek, Storm Lake to North Twin to Easter, then Lake Ahquabi."

Could this really be happening? Shivers started running down my back, and it was still close to a hundred outside. Skimming the

Placerville article, three bodies had been discovered. The article stated the bodies were disfigured but one was thought to be that of a girl of fourteen. One year younger than me. Three years younger than Shilo.

I gave Pitts back the papers and gave him a nod, then headed over to my bike. Pitts mounted his. "Hey, where're we going?" Diddleman asked. "Let's go to the Queen. I'm starving."

Chewbacca started following us out of the drive and I had to stop and order him back. I waited until he'd gone back to the porch, circled the old rug before finally slumping down and putting his paws on his feet.

But we weren't going to the Queen. Pitts and I took lead. We were going to Eagles Park.

As we rode, Pitts told about how a girl was missing in Dubuque. Several kids plus an old man found dead in Cedar Rapids. A woman reported missing in Mason City. It seemed like people were turning up dead and girls were missing everywhere.

I told him about the cow mutilation at the Martin place and what Officer Hayworth told me. We turned off Main and took the street out to Highway 99.

"Hold on, you guys. This isn't the way to the Queen," Diddleman yelled. "Where're you going? Hold it...Don't tell me ..." Diddleman didn't finish. He didn't need to.

It was where the scientist in Pitts urged him to go to get more intel, and the storyteller in me needed to go in order to make any sense of what was happening.

CHAPTER FOUR

We were worn out by the time we got there. Not that we couldn't bike the seven miles from Pinkerton to Eagles Park, but in that type of heat- one mile felt like ten. The park encompassed about a thousand acres with three major campgrounds and many campsites. One main entrance led to the lake, but there were many back roads to camping sites and hiking trails.

A camper's paradise, the park had something for the whole family. The lake was good fishing with bass, northern pike, tiger muskie, channel catfish, bluegill, crappie. The picnic grounds offered play equipment for when the kids got tired of swimming. For the more athletic visitors, there were challenging hills for hikers, nature trails, a handful of caves for exploring, bridle trails. Mostly, people just liked relaxing under the towering white oaks, some more than three hundred years old.

The lake, found in the center of all of it, was said to be on a list as one of the deepest lakes in the United States, although I'm not sure anyone ever measured it. It could have been an old wives' tale to keep kids closer to the edge rather than taking the challenge of swimming across at the widest part.

The main entrance is quickest to the lake, but we didn't get far, for two County Sheriff's cars were parked in front of the information kiosk. Spotting us, one officer immediately shouted, "Lake's closed today, boys."

"What's going on?" I yelled, wanting it to appear like we'd just come down for a swim.

"When's it going to open back up?" Pitts added.

"Not for a good while. Now you boys get yourselves back to town."

Pitts glanced at me and I gave him an answering nod. Diddleman whined, "No you guys. If I get into trouble…."

Without another word, we left and turned our bikes around as if we were headed back the same way. As soon as we were sure we couldn't be seen, we jumped off the bikes and hid them in the brush. We took off on foot, running parallel to the parkway road leading to the parking lot, picnic grounds and boat ramp.

The sighting of a deer stopped us, fast. A young white-tailed deer, it's eyes had been poked out by buzzards, entrails spilled out.

"Oh God, I think I'm gonna puke." Diddleman began making retching sounds.

"This is worse than the cow I found," I told Pitts.

Pitts went in for a closer look. "I've read about farmers finding cows with utters cut off. Or cattle castrated. Nothing like this. This looks like someone gutted it for fun and then left it to die."

He circled around the deer then squatted next to it so he could get a better look. "I don't think this is alien-related. Mutilations associated with aliens aren't sloppy like this. In fact, veterinarians and surgeons who have studied alien-mutilations have been impressed with the meticulous precision used.

He stood and scratched his head, thinking aloud. "Doesn't make sense. From what I've read, aliens seem to be studying how people and animals are sexually linked. The Hills' couple who were abducted reported how his private parts were studied, and the aliens put a needle into her belly button." He tuned to me. "Either they have this sex-thing figured out and now they are trying to understand how our bodies are different or they're experimenting in a whole 'nother way."

I didn't like linking the cow I'd seen with the deer because what popped into my head next was Officer Wilcox. "You said Wilcox was punctured in the chest?" Pitts must have been thinking of Wilcox, too. He nodded. "I overhead Mom telling Dad that he died from blood loss. He'd been punctured in the chest. She would never have told me. I'm too young to be hearing and seeing stuff like this."

Pitts said, "I bet this is only the start of what we're going to find."

"Hey, you guys. You can't be serious. Are you saying that aliens from another planet landed at Eagles? "

Pitts turned on Diddleman. "Why not? An alien ship crashed at Roswell in 1947. They're probably in every state. A lot more places than Pinkerton."

Of course, I didn't stop to remind Pitts that Diddleman didn't share our reading enthusiasm. He was more of a picture-type of guy.

Pitts continued. "Everyone knows presidents have been in on the cover up. The CIA, dude, they conceal intelligence on aliens because most people like you'd pee your pants if you saw one. President Bush was head of the CIA. He's part of the Majestic Twelve Group. That's the division than manages UFOs. Roswell wasn't the beginning." He went over and poked Diddleman in the chest as he passed him. "Wake up, dude. They're real. And they're here."

Diddleman began looking around, eyes wide. "Here?"

"Who knows? Maybe there are aliens in the CIA. Maybe they make up some of the Majestic Twelve. They're probably hiding right out in the open."

Diddleman checked around again. "Shit." His eyes bugged out of his head as if an alien at any moment was going to jump out from behind the nearest tree. "Is that them making that sound?"

Pitts and I gave a listen. "What sound?" I asked.

"That hum. Don't you hear it?"

I gave it another listen. Nothing. "You can go back, if you want, Diddleman. Just don't tell anyone where you've been." I followed Pitts.

It was more than a few minutes before I heard tromping coming up behind me. "Hold on, you guys. Wait up."

The trees started to thin out telling us we were getting closer to the lake. It's when I started hearing the hum Diddleman had mentioned. It was a low buzz, like when you stand under power lines.

We moved to the edge of the clearing, close to the picnic grounds dotted with wooden tables, cast iron barbecues and an area with swings and jungle bars. City and county cars were parked in the lot, some with their lights off, others whirling red and blue. Standing on a slight rise gave us a good view to the lake, where I made out Sheriff Boggs. He was a hard man to miss. He stood alongside Chief Moore in his blue uniform and a guy in tan pants and a blue shirt, sleeves rolled to the elbows, carrying a black case. I recognized the third as Dr. Potter, the medical examiner for the county.

Pitts squatted down and motioned for me and Diddleman to do the same. We watched as the three men at the dock exchanged conversation. Officers in the parking lot stood in groups waiting for instructions or writing on the clipboards they held. County and City were intermingled. Usually they kept pretty separate since there was no love between Chief Moore and Sheriff Boggs. Cops can be really competitive when it comes to police matters. But not today. Not here. Not now.

A low ache pulled up in my head and the middle of my forehead began to throb, adding to the pulsing in my ears. Pitts started crawling forward on his belly. Diddleman and I did the same. We wormed our way up as close as we could get without coming totally out in the open. The closer we got, the more my head began to throb.

I searched over the parking lot. No electrical poles. No wires. Security light wires had been buried underground. Where was that humming coming from? I thought maybe it came from the police cars, many still running, as if at any time there'd be a need to jump in and take off after someone. But the droning thrum sounded more as if coming from above, where clouds covered the sky, bellies dark with rain.

"What's wrong?" Pitts asked.

"You hear that?"

"What?"

"A low buzzing."

"I told you guys," Diddleman stated.

Pitts listened, shook his head. "I don't hear anything."

I rubbed my forehead, the center above my nose feeling like it was swelling. The throbbing in my ears worsened. My shoulders began to ache. I stretched and cracked my neck.

"You okay?" Pitts asked again.

I blew it off. "Diddleman's got me hearing things now. I'm getting a headache. Probably the low pressure."

"I'm telling you, it's out there."

"I thought you didn't believe in aliens?" Pitts challenged him.

"I don't. But I can feel trouble coming a mile a minute. We're going to get caught and I'm going to catch hell."

"Not if you stay quiet, choad. And keep your head down."

"We should go back." Diddleman continued to argue.

"Shhh," Pitts waved him quiet, lowering his body to the ground. "Down you guys. Someone's coming."

"I'm screwed," Diddleman moaned.

What if we got caught? Pitts and I would be grounded for the rest of our lives. But Diddleman, if his dad was drunk, he'd kill Diddleman. Once his dad took after him in the front yard and Diddleman was yelling bloody hell. The neighbors thought this time Mr. Forester was definitely going to kill his own child. They called the police.

"Don't worry," I whispered over to Diddleman. "Just keep your head down." I decided to show myself before I'd let Diddleman and Pitts get caught. Or I'd jump up and start running so the police would be pulled away from where we hid. I wasn't brave or anything. It's just that when you don't have any brothers, only a sister, your friends become as close as brothers. Maybe even closer.

Pitts and I were closer than he and his brother, Jimmy. He told me Jimmy barely acknowledged he was alive. I'd have done anything for Pitts and Diddleman. Especially Diddleman. Our dads would chew our butts good, but Diddleman's dad was too sick to understand the hurt he was causing his son. And I'm not talking about any beating.

A city cop walked up close to where we hid and unzipped to take a piss. We were so close to him, I could smell his stream. Another cop walked up. Maybe he had the same on his mind. How'd we get trapped in a piss-hole? But the second one stopped short, and instead, offered a cigarette out of his pack. Both men lit up.

"Hell of a thing," the relieved cop said after lighting up off the other's Bic. "You ever hear of someone cuttin' out someone's heart?"

Pitts and I exchanged wide-eyed glances. He had to be talking about Officer Wilcox. Diddleman's eyes were totally bugged.

The cop put his cigarette pack back in his pocket. He took a drag, exhaling slow so that the smoke came out in a thin line. "Only a crazy person could do something like this."

"Or someone all drugged up." The other cop stated.

"Nah, this is demented. Not even a meth-head would cut out someone's insides. We're talking out of this world."

Pitts' eyebrow slowly raised.

They finished their smokes pretty much in silence, looking down towards the dock where the Sheriff and Chief Moore still stood. Then they smashed out their smokes, picking up their stubs and moved off together.

Diddleman eyes were about ready to fall out of his head. He almost blew it for us when he couldn't keep quiet any longer. "Oh my God. The aliens cut out Officer Wilcox's heart!"

"Shhh, quiet down before they hear you. Besides, that doesn't figure." Pitts' glasses had fallen clear down to the end of his nose, and his fingers were twitching. "They'd want to understand how we breed. But a heart? Biologically they'd have to have one themselves, or an organ like it to pump blood to the brain." He checked his glasses with his index finger. "Did you know if someone's head is cut off, there is probably enough blood in the brain to still keep cognitive functions working? Even though the heart's been ripped out, there would still be blood in the brain. Wilcox may have seen the alien close-up."

Pitts and I shared in the envy. I rubbed my forehead, the pain swelling big time.

I glanced down at the men on the dock. Aliens? In Pinkerton? It was hard to believe. Cool, like reading a science fiction story, but it couldn't be real. I'd been to Eagles Park a thousand times.

Yet, I had been to Eagles and I'd never heard this hum before, never got a headache. I then thought of the story Max Lamott told me as a kid. It was here the lake created a natural inlet where you could get easily close to the water. This must have been where the Indian woman came to bathe. Is this where the brave had his own heart ripped out?

My eyes traveled then moved to the other side of the lake, along the lake's rim, and caught movement. Templeton. He was pretty far away, but I knew it was him, although he wasn't wearing a hat. He was sitting on a log, clearly in view, watching what was going on. This must have been where he was coming when mom and I saw him.

"Teddy."

Pitts followed where I was looking. "What's he doing here?"

I told them about seeing him earlier.

"The guy's a freak," Diddleman spat. "Doesn't surprise me he's here. Why don't they arrest him?"

"Templeton didn't do this," Pitts stated.

"Templeton wouldn't hurt bugs," I defended him. "Besides, Wilcox could have fought him off. He doesn't weigh much."

Diddleman returned. "He don't hurt bugs, he eats bugs." He raised his right hand. "Swear to God. I watched him put a sow bug in his mouth like it was an M&M."

Pitts agreed with me. "You're off your rocker."

Diddleman wasn't convinced. "He's one of them. I'd bet you."

I did wonder…if we could see Templeton, then Sheriff Boggs and Chief Moore could clearly see him, too. Probably some of the cops in the parking lot had spotted him. After all, some of them were looking in his direction. But they didn't yell for him to get the hell out, like they had us.

A zing of pain stabbed like a brain freeze. A light, the purest white light I'd ever seen, arrowed out of the clouds seeming to aim straight at me."

"You guys. What's that?"

CHAPTER FIVE

"What?"

"That light."

"Where?"

I pointed over toward the lake. It was gone.

Diddleman and Pitts chorused, "I don't see anything."

But it had been there. I'd have sworn to it. A zinging pain again stabbed inside my head. I gave a yowl.

Pitts placed a hand on my shoulder. "Shhh. You okay, man?"

"My head. The light."

Pitts, always methodical, said, "Describe it."

"Brilliant, white, like a super light bulb turned on."

He played the skeptic. "It could have been lightning."

But there had been no thunder. I shook my head. I knew it wasn't lightning. "This was small. Round, not ragged."

I went to rub my forehead again and realized my headache was gone. I listened. My ears were no longer throbbing. The droning thrum was gone, too.

We sat watching until the police began to leave. Chief Moore came up from the dock along with Dr. Potter. They exchanged some conversation then both went to their separate cars. Dr. Potter's car headed out first, then the Chief behind him. City and county cars began pulling out of the lot, heading back up and around to the main exit.

We stayed and watched Sheriff Boggs as he stood a long time out on the dock by himself staring out across the lake. Was he watching Teddy? Did he also wander what Teddy was doing at the crime scene? I followed his head's movement, peering down the lake where the camping grounds were located, slowly up the other way where land and trees came down to the water's edge.

If you climbed up from there, you'd cross hiking trails and bridle trails webbed in and through, back and forth, up into the hills. The three of us had hiked them. Most all kids from Pinkerton had at one time or another.

When Boggs returned to the parking lot, he stopped to talk to a couple of officers before he got in his car. Guess those guys got the night shift.

We left the way we'd come, keeping bent over until we were sure we were out of sight from the parking lot. Pitts wanted to stop and inspect the deer again, but it was getting way too dark, fast. I was worried that if we didn't get back, we might have trouble finding our bikes.

We didn't travel more than a couple miles down the highway before it started raining. At first it was just a drop or two, then the clouds opened their bellies, and it sheeted rain in wind gusts. Thunder clapped and rumbled, like a huge bowling ball dropping and rolling across an old wooden alleyway.

My shirt was stuck to my back by the time we reached Main Street. My hair plastered to my head. Pitts had taken off his glasses. Diddleman wasn't complaining about the pace. Each boom of thunder pushed our legs to the limit.

Mom opened the door before my hand reached the knob. "Where the heck have you been?"

"Sorry. I was at Pitts and time got …."

"I know good and well you weren't at the Pitts' or the Foresters', so don't you even start. Their moms are ready to tear up both of their tails, too."

She wasn't one to get as mad as a wet hen, except when one of her chicks might get caught out in a storm. I didn't know both chicks were missing until she asked, "Do you know where Shilo is?"

My sister Shilo was going to be a senior next year, and my mom was hell-bent on both of us going to college. She kept a good eye on us, but lately, she'd been keeping more of an eye out on Shilo, saying things like Shilo was getting boy-crazy and she'd better watch herself. When Shilo sneaked in late the other night, heading straight to her room, Mom followed her up the stairway wanting to know where she'd been, who with, and warning her she wasn't too old for a *good paddlin'*. An event mom had been threatening since we were kids but rarely ever administered.

I wanted to be helpful. Knowing where Shilo might be was a way for me to get out of Dutch. I offered a pretty good guess. "Did you call over to Mr. Overhouser's place?"

Her eyes narrowed.

The Overhousers lived a couple blocks down the street. I'd overheard Shilo earlier in the day talking with Blake Overhouser, and when I went to get a haircut, I caught sight of her getting into his Dodge pickup at the corner of our block. Mom had nothing against the Overhousers, but she had a serious aversion to how Blake drove his pickup. She said he was like to kill himself and anyone else trying to cross the street. She'd also heard gossip about his drinking and partying at Eagles. I'd heard the same, but with envy.

I knew Mom would be fit to be tied with the thought of Shilo with Blake, but I didn't expect her to rip out of the door into the storm in her house slippers. Chewbacca ran out after her before I could stop him. Thunder blasted and rolled as they took off down the street. Electric fingers raked the clouds. "Hey mom, I was joking," I yelled. "She's probably over at Gloria's."

I was just about to run after her when dad pulled me back in. "Where are you goin'?"

"Mom's headed to the Overhousers'."

"Why's she going to the Overhousers'?"

"She thinks Shilo's there."

"What would Shilo be doing at their place?" My dad may be an engineer working for the NASA space program, but sometimes he wasn't good at putting the simplest things together. "All thumbs," is how mom described him.

I decided not to go into it. He began rubbing his forehead. "Get in the house. Your mother can take care of herself." He shut the door.

Boom!

Another thunder ball slammed onto the Pinkerton alleyway. The glass in the windows shook. *Crackkkkkk.* Lightning lit up the room. The storm, like a great beast with sharp teeth, was not going to be denied. It'd waited long enough.

"Get the flashlights and candles in case we lose electricity. I'll call the Overhousers and tell your mom to stay there until the storm passes. Don't forget to unhook the TV and computers."

I ran around the house getting flashlights, finding candles and matches. Usually we didn't need them, but as mom would say, better to be safe than sorry.

One time when a bad storm went through when I was little, it stormed so bad the wind pulled off the roofing and broke enough wires we had to use candles. We cooked with the barbecue for three days. Of course, I *was* a little kid then, and I thought it was all fun. However, I had an uncanny feeling this was not going to be a good time.

I heard dad talking on the phone. It sounded like mom found Shilo and she wasn't happy. Which meant Shilo wasn't going to be happy, either. If mom forgot to give me hell, Shilo would. Payback's a bitch.

I unplugged the television downstairs and retreated upstairs to my room, thinking the best thing for me was to go to bed and pretend to be asleep. Innocent as can be. The wind had picked up, yowling down the street. I unplugged my computer and then checked out the window. The trees in the front yard were bending at forty-five degree angles and the taller ones in front of the street lights made for an eerie flickering.

Thunder resounded overhead. Fiery fingers from hell streaked out of the clouds.

Then everything blacked out.

Another slice of light, this time so close to the Cox's house roof across from ours, it struck, sending sizzling sparks along the roof line. Close. Too close.

I knew I wasn't supposed to stand near a window when there was lightning. A fork of lightning can break glass. But I couldn't move. Then *clash*. The sound of another flash of light. This time it was so great it lit the entire neighborhood. I saw Teddy Templeton. He was sitting across the street in a lawn chair, legs crossed, easy-like, as if he were waiting for a parade to come down the street. He saw me see him, and he took off his hat and waved it.

What the hell?

My ears began popping.

An ice-freeze jolt stabbed my brain, like it had at Eagles. I gripped my head with both hands. Piercing pain spread, swelling, until I worried my head was about to explode. I squeezed my eyes closed to force the pain back. Then I heard another sound, a screeching wail. And in the darkness of my closed eyes, I saw a white light. Small and scattered at first, the light grew together as if focusing between my eyes. At times so direct, so piercing, so brilliant, so white. Whiter than anything I'd ever seen. The light between my eyes began to pulse to the rhythm pounding in my head. It stabbed over and over again, cutting my head apart, one piece at a time.

I screamed for it to stop. "Let me go!"

"What are you doing?" Dad's voice. He moved as if in slow motion. His legs first, then his body catching up, arms swinging as if he were swimming in a pool of air. His mouth moved, but I couldn't hear him. It was as if we were a universe apart instead of the few steps separating us.

As he got closer, a string of color exploded, one color after another. Greens, blues, deep reds and brilliant yellows, gold. They swirled around him in waves, bending, arcing into each other, making purple, crimson, stretching from him to me, shrinking back to him.

Crackkkkkkkkkkkkkkk.

At the sound the colors dissolved but with their withdrawal the sounds of all eternity exploded. Voices murmuring. But they were speaking in a strange language I didn't recognize. And I heard horrible pronouncements of death, hell, anger, my voice, their voice, words of suffering, screams of anguish. All was shrill and faint except for a dull drumming sound pounding in my head, my ears, my gut.

Dad's voice loudest. "Get in the basement."

"But…"

"You want to get killed? A tornado's been spotted."

A siren screamed a shrilling, high-pitched, ear-splitting, shriek.

"Dad, what's going on? I don't understand."

"It's a tornado, Jake. Get in the basement. NOW."

I twisted, checking out the window, thinking I should yell for Templeton to come with us. Then I saw mom and Shilo. Shilo was wearing the sky blue blouse she'd been wearing when she got into the truck with Buck. Chewbacca was there, too, sitting at Mom's feet. Mom had a hold of Shilo's shoulders like she wanted to push her to get home. Like Shilo was still refusing. Then Shilo yelled something. She was looking back toward the Overhousers'.

Something dark was moving across Pinkerton. It lumbered above the house roofs like a low-burdened cloud, low, lower. Lightning streaked out of it. No, not lightning, a beam.

A circle of yellowed light encircled Mom and Shilo. Their bodies stiffened, like when we were kids and played statue. Chewbacca started barking. Then I thought I saw someone else with them. At first I thought it was Templeton, maybe having seen them he'd come over. Teddy liked my mom. But while the silhouette reminded me of Templeton, this person appeared smaller.

I expected Mom to grab Shilo and whoever it was and start marching them to the house. But instead, she glanced at my window. It's like she knew I was watching.

The darkness consumed them as the light diminished, and in its place flew a rotating ball of radiant light, so stunning it should have burnt my eyes blind like the sun. Like in a movie, it glided toward me, rising higher, closer, coming within an arm's length away. Softly it glowed. I was so mesmerized by this ball of light that I yearned to reach out to touch it.

Come.

The pain in my head began to recede as the word stirred my fears. *Come.* The world's noise quieted. Was this a dream? Was I awake? Asleep? Then I heard another voice. Not dad's. Not mom's or Shilo's. Not from the outside. It came from my thoughts. A voice like mine but one I thought I knew.

Jakob.

With the sound of my name, the entire world burst into color, so pure, humming low, my name called over and over again, *Jakob.* The brilliant globe shrank smaller and smaller, becoming a speck of glowing illumination before opening the darkness as doors open to an elevator, offering a pathway through parted clouds.

Come. Home.

"Jake." Dad's voice.

I knew I should go to him, but this pull of my imagination, this magical delusion was as great as when he and I would lay on the lawn late at night and gaze up at the stars. While we would lay still, in all the quiet of the night, I'd hear the quiet, unintelligible sounds of people from opened windows, the sounds of insects and night birds, and feel the stars fall toward the Earth as I moved further into space. I asked dad if he felt it too, the connection between there and here. He'd said there was no real separation between any and all of it. It was all one. I was one.

At this moment, standing in my bedroom with the sounds of booming thunder and the cracks of light splitting the dark, along with the pain in my head so encompassing it felt as if it was not my skull but my mind already shattered in a million pieces, I thought I understood what my Dad had meant.

"Jake, what's got into you?" He grabbed my arm. At first I fought him. Wasn't he listening, couldn't he see? I understood everything, as if my mind knew every answer to every question. I twisted away and rushed to the window, ready to take the elevator, follow Mom and Shilo to where ever the dream turned into reality beyond the stars.

But there was no longer an opening. Just the dead of darkness.

"Jake. Now!"

"Dad! No! "

He forced out me out of the room, down the stairs. I tried to tell him. "Outside. Mom. Shilo."

"They're at the Overhousers."

I slipped and fell at the bottom of the stairwell. He jerked me onto my feet. "No, they're…" Half carrying me, we went through to the kitchen. He opened the basement door, almost throwing me down the steps.

Thock, thock.

Hail like a soft hammer began hitting the house. My ears began to ache. An ice-piercing pain punctured my forehead once again. Then a sledgehammer took over.

BAM BAM.

The house shook as the wind howled for destruction, reverberating over and around, a monster screeching as a rumbling, heavy train moving on its path. The basement filled with dust, spiraling, suffocating, blinding.

Come!

"Dad!"

"Get under here." He shoved me hard under the heavy flooring where the old kitchen had once been built. Wood cracked. Glass broke.

"Keep your head down."

Claws grated on the side of the house. The monster's sharp teeth bit into whatever was decayed, wanting more and more, until I thought it would gulp down the house in one huge bite, then sink its teeth into dad and me.

"Jake, look out!!"

I went with the light into the dark.

Come

Home.

The last thing I heard was my Dad. "Jake? Jake? Don't you leave me."

CHAPTER SIX

When I opened my eyes, it took a couple of seconds to remember where I was and why. Dad's face was streaked in dirt and tears. I guess he thought I'd died or something.

"Can you move?"

"Yeah. I think so." The back of my head hurt, and when I did move, it felt like my brain clunked against my skull.

"Slowly. You okay?"

"Yeah." I got on my feet.

Neither of us knew what we'd find when we went back up the basement steps. Opening the door into the kitchen, dad swung his flashlight around. Everything was as we left it. The mixing bowls set on the counter where mom had been baking. A pan stood on the stove, supper started. The smell of hamburger and fried onions filled the room. Nothing had fallen.

"Whew, I thought for sure we got it," Dad said. His hand squeezed my shoulder. "The house shook enough to dislodge that post on you. Are you sure you're okay?"

"I think so."

"I've got a thunderclap headache from the barometric pressure." He rubbed his forehead. "I sure wish your mom had come home." He headed towards the living room and the front door. "Let's go get them."

"They were outside when the storm hit," I told him, remembering, and trying again to tell him what I saw.

He stopped. "What?"

"I saw them. I tried to tell you."

"Jake, you're mistaken. Your mom promised me she'd stay at the Overhousers until the storm passed."

"They were outside."

He squeezed my shoulder again. "You passed out. You must have dreamed it. They're at the Overhousers."

Was it all a dream?

I wanted it to be.

Outside, the world appeared unearthly. Smoke curled, hazed white against gray, replacing the clouds, where house roofs should have been. Night ended, evening returned.

As far as I could see, every house seemed destroyed.

Every house, but ours.

"Dad?" Was I still dreaming? "What's happened? Why is ours the only house left standing?"

He didn't answer.

His silence told me. This wasn't a dream. This was a living nightmare.

Those who'd somehow escaped their wrecked houses were walking around broken wires, fallen trees, scattered wood and someone's bathtub setting out in the middle of the street. They moved like zombies--staggering, eyes wide, mouths open. On one lawn, a group of women clung together, their children crying. On another, men stood, arms hanging helplessly at their sides.

"Dad?"

"Stay here, Jake." He stepped forward out into the street, and when he did, it was as if the world turned back on. He and others rushed over to Howard and Beth Cox's place across from ours.

"Over here. They're trapped." A voice called out.

"I hear her. Beth?" Another voice shouted.

I followed. Together we lifted off torn roofing and heavy beams. Beth's new General Electric stove with duel burners had been picked up and placed against their basement door as tidily as if placed there by hand.

"Is Beth all right? Is Howard with her?" Whispers.

"They're okay." The chant came down the line of us standing waiting for the outcome.

"I can hear them," someone closer to the front yelled.

"We're okay."

"They're okay."

A collective sigh of relief came when Howard Cox poked his sandy red head out of the doorway. "Glad to see you, boys." He smiled. Beth came out behind him. They were both unharmed. When Beth saw her new General Electric, at first she seemed happy to see it wasn't damaged, but then as she noticed how most of her house was gone, she said she wished she'd have kept her old one.

A chorus of shouting echoed throughout the neighborhood.

The men took off to help at another house. I wanted to follow them, but my head began hurting so bad, I had to sit down at the curb.

Only a fireplace wall remained where there had once been a house next to ours. And next to it, old Mrs. Hansen, her dress dirty and torn, stood in front of a flattened structure saying to no one next to her, "What happened to my house?"

I felt something drip down my jaw line. My fingers brushed at the wetness, blood. My ear was bleeding.

I tried to replay in my mind what I'd seen. Mom and Shilo coming home. Something stopping them. But the memory flickered like a television getting a bad signal. Dad must have been right. It was all a dream. That meant, I'd see them any moment. Mom'd be hurrying home, worried to death about dad and me.

I couldn't see as far as the Overhouser's. Was it still standing like ours? Or smashed into a heap like the Cox's?

I got up. They should have been here by now. I went to go meet them.

My stomach heaved. My vision blurred. I sat back down.

I searched for dad. Had they found him? I could see a group of men three houses further up the block and thought he must be with them. But there was no sign of Mom. The smell of smoke grew heavier. If she didn't show soon, I'd go get dad. Together we'd go on down to the Overhouser's. What if they'd been trapped inside, too?

An explosion sounded. Police and fire sirens wailed in the distance. Suddenly, I couldn't wait. Feeling as if I was on a boat in choppy water, I walked slowly, keeping to the middle of the street, keeping an eye out for live wires, broken glass, stepping over branches, house-siding and roof shingles, some with nails still intact. A dog lay twisted with its head crushed in. I thought of Chewbacca.

Trees had been pulled up by their roots or stood standing with branches splintered and twisted and every leaf missing. A washing machine stood planted on a lawn and a woman was pulling out her wash. As if the cycle was done and she needed to get her clothes out on the line.

"Chewbacca?" I yelled.

People were rescuing each other, like we'd helped our neighbors. They called out names.

"Mom? Shilo?"

Families were taking count, making sure everyone was accounted for. More sirens. The entire town screamed angrily.

I came up to the Overhouser's house. I stumbled on what should have been a sidewalk. House parts had been pitched about. Mad panic, however, didn't set in until I saw Mr. Overhouser stooped over like someone had punched him in the gut.

"Mom?! Shilo?!" I ran, screaming. Thinking, *They must be trapped. I need to get them out.* But out from where? Barely a foundation remained.

"Hold on there. Jake, what're you doin' here?" Ike Overhouser grabbed a hold of me as I raced past him "Where's your folks?"

"Help me. I need to get mom out." Why didn't he know? "Shilo. They're trapped."

"You're mom? She ain't here, son. Aren't she and your sister at your place?"

Stunned, I stared at him. "They stayed with you."

His expression worried. "Are you telling me your mom didn't make it home?" He glanced away, mumbling, "I knew I shouldn't have let her leave."

Blake came up holding his arm. Mabel Overhouser appeared asking, "What are we going to do? Not one house is left standing."

There was one house on the street left standing, but I didn't mention which one.

"Jake here's looking for his mom."

"You're mom? Why, she went home before the storm hit." Her eyes widened realizing if my mom had gotten home then I wouldn't be out looking for her. Her tone softened. "Now, don't you worry, Jake. Your mom probably ducked into someone else's house hearing those sirens. You'll find them."

But I knew. I heard it inside of me, a voice telling me that the storm had taken them. If not the storm, then something else.

Still, I went from one disaster to the next searching for them, hoping at any moment to hear my mom's voice say something like, *Jake, what are you doing? Get home.* Looking forward to seeing Shilo, madder than hell that I'd given up her secret rendezvous. *You just wait, Jake. You'll be sorry.* And that would be okay by me. I wouldn't have cared.

I didn't want this nightmare to be real. *Please, let it all be a dream.*

Two neighborhoods were hit, ours and the next block over. It was Howard Cox that stated the tornado created a landing strip. Out of all the houses in those two neighborhoods, ours was the only one still completely intact and standing. There was no reasoning it. Although there were some who stopped to observe and comment to Howard and Beth. They saw the difference between their homes and ours but said that strange things happen all the time.

I told dad what the Overhousers told me, and we went from house to house checking to see if Mabel Overhouser's suggestion might be true. That mom and Shilo had slipped into someone's house before getting to ours and they just hadn't gotten around as yet. Coming up empty, we continued searching, walking the several blocks to the high school where the gym was turned into a shelter. Cots set up. Tables placed where people brought food. The Red Cross, white jackets with blood red crosses, stood providing information and directions. Nurses, both in uniform and out, guided those hurt over to where they could receive first aid.

Not finding them at the gym, dad thought he should go on over to the hospital. "You're mom's probably helping out." It did sound like something she would do. Or knowing her, she would have gone home and heated up the oven, preparing to feed the entire city.

Only, I couldn't reason with him that she would start helping others before she'd known everything was all right at home. She would have needed to see dad and me for herself. Look us over to make sure we were okay. Not finding her at the school was bad news.

But neither of us were ready to admit that if she wasn't here it could mean she and Shilo were hurt. Or worse. It wasn't a dream.

"I want you to stay right here." He pointed to the floor in front of my feet as if an "X" marked the spot. "I don't want to have to look for you and them. Besides, they'll come here just like we did."

"I want to go with you."

I turned over onto my side.

Was Chewbacca with them? Or was he dead, too? And why hadn't I remembered he was with them? I could have told Dad and maybe hearing that Chewbacca was there, too, would have made it all the more real.

I had a sense that more happened than I was telling. A pain, headache? Colors? A voice calling?

The shame that I did nothing to save them overpowered any clear memory of the events.

Why had I just stood there? I was a coward?

I felt a hand on my shoulder. The tears came.

Diddleman's voice cracked. "Don't worry, man. I'm sure they're all right. We should find Templeton. I bet that freak knows where they are."

Then I heard the click of the cube and Pitts thinking out loud. "What you're saying makes sense. I've read articles where lots of people who witnessed a UFO or who said they were abducted felt like they couldn't move. And afterwards, they couldn't remember anything until they were put under hypnosis."

Then he believed me?

As Pitts' voice drifted further and further away, I thought how I really wished it was a UFO because if it was then mom and Shilo would be still alive. The aliens might let them go.

"What time is it?" I asked when I woke up.

Diddleman was sitting in his chair thumbing a Gameboy. "Hey, you're back." He came over, jumping on the bed, walking around me like a crazy person saying he'd thought I was going to die. Pitts joined him. Not by jumping on the bed, of course. Not Pitts' style. But both were glad to have me with them. I was pretty happy to be there, too. It was the first time I'd really slept since the night of the storm.

"Stop it, you guys." I got out of bed and hurried to the bathroom, knocking several things over as I veered from the path.

When I got back, Pitts told me I'd slept for more than twenty-four hours. That while he shook me, his mom worrying because I wasn't eating, but no matter how much he shook me, he couldn't get me to wake up. Finally, I guess, his dad said just to let me sleep.

The three of us went downstairs for breakfast. When I'd taken my seat, Mrs. Pitts set a plate in front of me. She put the back of her hand to my forehead and remarked how I didn't have a fever, as if she was surprised I wasn't sick. She also mentioned how I'd almost worried her to death.

I plowed into the eggs and bacon while Pitts and his parents caught me up. His dad had gone looking for mine but couldn't find anyone who had seen him. Then Pitts mom continued where his Dad left off, telling me she thought he was at the hospital "Now, Jake, we don't want you to worry."

Which caused me to immediately worry.

"I haven't actually seen him, so I could be wrong, but I'm pretty sure I overhead his nurse say his name. Dr. Potter is his doctor and he brought in someone from the outside to work as the patient's private nurse."

She said to Mr. Pitts more than to us, "Which didn't go down very well with many of us, I can tell you that."

She turned back to me. "Emily Cotter said she heard the patient's a burn victim, and that takes specialized nursing. But when I asked if it was your dad, she said the patient hadn't been listed on the patient file yet."

A burn victim? He'd been hurt? How badly? My face must have shown my confusion and horror, for she quickly added. "That's why calling in a specialized nurse is a good thing, hon. He's getting the best of care. Don't worry. Everything is going to be all right. I'm sure of it. I am sorry I don't know any particulars. The hospital is full and all of us are working double shifts." She paused. "This is probably all sounding worse than it is, but it's all I know. He's marked as 'no visitors,' but I'm sure that won't mean you."

I got up from the table. "I need to go see him."

"Finish your breakfast first," Mr. Pitts said.

"You need to get your strength back. I'll take you as soon as you're done and ready," Mrs. Pitts said, telling me she was on the late morning shift and needed to leave in a little bit.

I sat back no longer hungry. I toyed with the balance of food on my plate. Her words, hospital, *burn patient*, repeating in my mind.

The conversation at the table changed from my dad to the other news around town. They talked about how in all the damage, only three people had died.

"That's really low for this kind of disaster." Mrs. Pitts got up from the table and went over to the counter, putting dirty dishes in the sink and rinsing them with water. Mr. Pitts followed her, handing her his plate.

It was Diddleman who said they found Palmer Dodd in his house. I knew the Dodd's didn't live in the storm track. They lived on the other side of the high school.

"But from a heart attack," Pitts clarified. Pitts went on. "Dave Stockman got caught out in the storm in his car. They found him in it five miles the other side of Pinkerton. Alive."

I got up and went over to Mr. and Mrs. Pitts, handing Mrs. Pitts my plate and silverware. "You haven't heard anything about my mom and sister?"

"No, Jake," Mrs. Pitts answered, adding. "I'm sorry."

"Can we go to the hospital right now? I really want to see my dad."

She and Mr. Pitts exchanged glances. She wiped her hands dry. "I'll go get ready. We'll leave right away."

The phone rang. "I'll get that." Mr. Pitts went out of the room.

A hard knocking rattled the back door. Mrs. Pitts opened it, and we all saw Tira Templeton standing on the porch. A large woman, her hair stood out wild from her head, as if she hadn't bothered combing it. And her clothes, always hanging large on an already large-frame, seemed wrinkled and crumpled more than normal.

She was breathing hard, her words short. "I'm lookin' for Teddy. Is he here?" She glanced around, over to the table at Diddleman and Pitts, then to me. "He didn't come home last night and I thought he might be here with the boys." Her eyes stayed on me. "Was he with you, Jake?"

"He hasn't been here, Tira." Mrs. Pitts answered for me.

She glanced nervously behind her shoulder as if having heard something, maybe thinking Teddy was coming up behind her, before she said, "I know he's usually with you boys. He's always talking about the three of you. If you know where he is, don't worry, I'm not angry. He's not going to be in trouble. I just want to make sure he's a all right."

I saw Diddleman roll his eyes. He whispered something over to Pitts and laughed.

Tira Templeton had heard. Her head sharply jerked back to the table. She frowned at Diddleman. She gave me a disappointed look that shamed me. "Especially you, Jake. He's always talking about you."

"Yeah, he's one of our best friends. Isn't he Jake?" Diddleman's voice dripped with sarcasm.

"That's enough, Walter." Mrs. Pitts reprimanded. "I'm sorry, Tira. We've been talking to Jake about his father. He may have been taken to the hospital. You know, his mom and sister haven't been found?"

"I hadn't heard about your father, Jake. I hope it's nothing serious. He's a nice man. He came out of his way to make sure Teddy and I were okay."

He went to the Templeton's'? Why?

Mrs. Pitts said to Diddleman. "Walter, you owe Mrs. Templeton an apology."

Diddleman turned his eyes away. "Sorry."

"Was Teddy with you the night of the storm?" If she said no, that I would know for sure it wasn't a dream. Teddy had been across the street.

But before his mom could answer, Mrs. Pitts embraced her. "I'm sorry. We really need to go, Tira. I'm on this morning's shift. But I'm sure Teddy's fine. I'll tell him to get on home when I see him."

"He is a sweet boy. He wouldn't hurt a fly." Tira Templeton said quietly.

"But I bet he's eaten a few." Diddleman whispered to Pitts, but this time not so loud that Pitts' mom or Teddy's could hear.

CHAPTER EIGHT

*N*one of us spoke as we got in the car and drove to the hospital. Pitts and Diddleman insisted on coming with me, although Pitts' mom told them they wouldn't be allowed in my dad's room. Not unless the doctor had changed the instructions for no visitors. "I'll look for you up on the floor, Jake. And Oliver? I expect all of you back at the house in a couple of hours. They're saying we could be in for more storms." She dropped us off at the lobby and continued on to park the car.

Pinkerton General wasn't that big. Maybe a hundred beds. Specialists from Des Moines came down when the local doctors couldn't treat, like for cancer or a heart bi-pass.

The lobby doors opened to an antiseptic smell as if it'd just been sprayed and cleaned by anti-bacterial shampoo. A handful of people filled the chairs. It was less than a week since the storm, but this room gave little sign of the disaster or emergency.

A volunteer was reading a magazine, *National Geographic*. The page was headlined, "Spitzer Space Telescope" and showed the Andromeda Galaxy." I'd already read it.

"Excuse me."

She was riveted onto the photo of the galaxy and didn't know I was standing in front of her. Usually I'd wait to be noticed, but with my dad close by after so many days absent, I was in no mood to be polite.

"We're here to see Bill Cahill."

She glanced from her magazine.

"Can you tell me which room he is in?"

She came across more like a librarian than a hospital nurse. She was wearing a sweater loosely placed across thin, rounded shoulders and glasses secured with a glittering, silver chain. The vase of flowers on the counter added to the powerfully sweet perfume she'd applied before coming to work.

She took her glasses off, letting them swing onto her chest. Apparently they weren't needed for computer reading. Her fingers tapped keys. "I'm sorry. We have no one here by that name."

"William Cahill," I amended. "Everyone calls him Bill. I'm his son."

She tapped again. "I'm sorry, I show no patient, a William or Bill Cahill."

I glanced over to Pitts, who came forward saying, "My mother is Katherine Pitts. She's a nurse here. She's the one who told Jake his dad was in the hospital. On her floor. Second."

Again the volunteer tapped keys, checked the screen carefully and said, picking up her glasses as if to go back to her magazine. "Sorry. Maybe he was discharged."

"Then he would have come back home," I argued.

My insistence aggravated her. "Boys, I'm really too busy. Why don't you go back home and get your parents to help you."

I rechecked the lobby and counted. Three old men sitting slouched in chairs, one snoring. Two women, knees together, talking quietly. If this was her idea of busy, then the overload from the storm must have blown her away.

"His PARENT is in the hospital!" Diddleman yelled so loud, every head in the room turned our way. Even the guy sleeping woke up.

Pitts pulled Diddleman away from the counter. I followed them. "What?" Diddleman was saying. "She wasn't helping."

"Yelling is only going to get us thrown out." Pitts warned.

Diddleman shrugged. "Whatever. Let's see *you* find his dad."

Pitts blew off the challenge. "Didn't my mom say something like she heard his name? Let's just go upstairs and find my mom. She'll figure this out." Pitts headed to the elevators. He pushed the button to the second floor. As we rode in the air-tight capsule, sounds and smells became void.

Pitts said to Diddleman, "What's got you so hostile?"

"She was jerking us around," Diddleman said.

"She wasn't jerking us around," Pitts defended. "She was doing her job."

"If she would have been doing her job, she would have gotten off her butt and went to find out why Jake's dad wasn't on the computer."

"Settle down, Diddleman." I knew he was just trying to support me, but his voice was pretty loud, and I didn't want the elevators to open on the second floor with anyone thinking we were some guys messing around.

A hospital can be nasal-suicide. The elevator opened to a crisis of unimaginable olfactory proportions: morning bowel movements, vomit, dirty bandages, unmade beds, breakfast.

Two nurses in colorful scrubs similar to what Pitts' mom had been wearing stood behind a Pepto Bismol-colored counter, clean and neat except for several closed notebooks, a small pile of file folders and a breakfast tray missed going back to the cafeteria with the others. One nurse was talking on the telephone, and the other, head turned, was speaking to someone in an opened doorway.

"Hi Ashley." The nurse turned around in her chair, curious who was saying her name. Her hair had been pulled back in a ponytail and she was wearing a button badge—"Have A Good Day!" with a smiley face—and a name tag identifying her as Ashley Paine. "Oliver, what are you doing here?" A little older than Pitts' brother Jimmy, I wasn't sure if she was a real nurse or more of a nurse's assistant taught a trade at the community college.

Pitts continued with the lead. "Can you let my mom know we're here?"

She glanced at an opened binder. "She hasn't logged in and I haven't seen her." She twisted in her swivel chair, calling to whoever stayed out of sight. "Janet, have you seen Katherine? Her son is here."

A voice, then a face, emerged from the room. It was Janet Evans. Phil Evan's mom, quarterback for the football team. "She's on shift, but I haven't seen her, yet."

"We know she's here," Pitts informed them. "We came with her. Can we wait?"

"Of course," Ashley said. "She should be right up."

"Jake needs to see his dad," Diddleman said.

"Shhhh…" Pitts warned.

"What?" Diddleman asked, unsure why he was again being shushed.

"Oh, is your dad a patient?" While I knew who Ashley was, or at least recognized her face—everyone pretty much has bumped into each other at one time or another in Pinkerton--she probably would have no idea who I was, or even my dad for that matter..

"Bill Cahill." I informed her. Then quickly added, "William Cahill."

She tapped on the computer keyboard. "We don't have a patient by that name on this floor."

Pitts and I exchanged glances. "We'll wait for mom," Pitts said.

We didn't have to wait long. Pitts' mom came from down the hallway, walking briskly toward us as if she was late. Several steps behind her walked Dr. Potter.

"Oliver? Jake?" Pitts' mom hesitated slightly, glancing back from where she'd come, then came straight to me saying, "I'm so sorry. I was mistaken, Jake. It wasn't your father after all." She again peeked over her shoulder, then corralled the three of us, leading us to the elevator. "Go on home, boys."

"But mom?" Pitts argued.

I saw Doctor Potter down the hall open a door and move inside. Two things I was sure of. First, Pitts' mom wasn't one to make mistakes. Especially a big one like this. She wouldn't have told me my dad was here unless she was pretty sure. Losing him after my mom and sister was about all I could handle. Second, it wasn't like her to be jittery, checking over her shoulder, hurrying us to the elevators as if we, or she, was doing something wrong.

"I need to go to the bathroom." I stepped away.

"You can use the bathroom in the lobby." She pushed the elevator button.

"Isn't there one on this floor?" I didn't wait for her to answer. I headed off as to seek one out.

"Jake, come back here."

I passed several rooms, seeing patients elevated watching television, nurses checking IV's, a supportive family member sleeping in a chair nearby the bed. Only two doors were closed. I played my hunch, my hand on the handle of the farthest one. I opened the door.

Immediately a smell punched me in the nose, reminding me of the time mom made Sloppy Joes for dinner and got talking on the phone, burning the entire batch.

Dr. Potter's stood with his back to me. A nurse, mask over her mouth and nose, was fiddling with the saline bags hooked above the bed where a person lay unclothed, skin red, and several areas blackened, like a piece of chicken kept too long on a barbecue.

The nurse noticed me and nodded. Dr. Potter checked her nod.

Unsure of what to do now that the moment had come, I said, "I'm Jake Cahill."

"So you are." He stood as if waiting for me to decide my next move.

I wasn't sure the person lying on the bed was my dad or someone else. I took a step forward.

"You can't come in here," the nurse warned.

Feet were big. Legs long. Moving closer, stepping to the right of Dr. Potter, the upper body came into view. Way too large a frame for a woman. The man's eyes were covered with gauze, his face so badly burned I couldn't detect a nose. How could this person still be alive?

Please, I thought, wishing now Pitts' mom was mistaken and this wasn't my father.

"This isn't…" the nurse began.

Dr. Potter moved aside. I came closer, trying to keep my eyes elsewhere, horrified. I glued them to the IV tube, generally placed in an arm but his too badly damaged, running under the thin white sheet covering the private areas of a body swollen, appearing at any moment it would burst.

"Dad?"

Fingers on one hand moved.

"Dad?" My voice cracked. God help me, I wasn't sure whether I wanted him to say, "Hi Jake, what's going on?" or "Sorry, kid, wrong person." I went to touch him, jerked back, repulsed, terrified.

. "Jake, this isn't your father. Come on. You're disturbing the patient." Dr. Potter said.

"It *is* my Dad. It's him."

I wanted to throw myself on him. Hug him to protect him. Fix him. Helpless. "Dad, it's me, Jake."

Dr. Potter took my arm. I jerked away. "This is Bill Cahill. My father."

Again, he grabbed me, this time taking a stronger grip. "Come on, son."

I faced him, tears running down my face, dripping off my chin. "Is he going to live?"

"I'm sorry to say, this man's prognosis isn't very good." Dr. Potter moved closer, lowered his voice. "He won't if you don't keep your mouth shut."

"What'd you say?" Had I heard him right? Had he just threatened me?

"I'll call for security." The nurse was already heading to the door.

"No. I'll take care of this." Dr. Potter left.

My brain didn't work like Pitts. I couldn't put the pieces together quickly. Why would Dr. Potter threaten me? I look at the man again. Everything about him, his size, the way he lay with his head slightly turned toward me, like when I was a little kid and I would come to wake him in the morning, thinking *I* was going to wake *him*.

"Boo!" he'd shout, scaring me.

His face, the face of my father, my dad, scarred, burned, gone. "Dad, it's me, Jake."

"Young man, don't you listen?" The nurse came around the bed and stood next to me. "Come away, right this minute. This man is highly susceptible…"

She reached out to grab my arm and pull me away. I raised my arm. She flinched as if I was going to hit her. Maybe I was. I was acting, not thinking.

"Where is Dr. Potter?" She hurried to the door.

I leaned down, closer. The smell of his burnt flesh churned my stomach, my throat tasted bile. I tried breathing through my mouth but worried if I kept it open, I might lose my breakfast.

"It's me, Dad. Jakob."

"I need this young man taken out of here immediately." Dr. Potter's voice.

"Yes, sir."

Security. The guard stepped towards me, arms held wide as if ready to tackle me. Then, I thought I heard my name. Faintly, but I was sure I heard it. I placed my hands as close to my dad's head as I dared. My lips as close to his skin as I thought I could without hurting him. "I'm here."

He whispered, "Boggs. Alive. Nest." At the last word, his body began jerking, jumping uncontrollably. The guard grabbed me. "Get your sorry ass out of here." He put a powerful grip on me, his forearm held against my neck, as he began forcing me out of the room.

As I moved past Dr. Potter, he growled, "What did he say to you?"

My eyes took in again the man on the bed clearly in convulsions. The nurse standing over him, injecting something into his IV tube.

"Did he say something?" Dr. Potter asked, louder.

"No." I made the word sound as full of despair as I felt. "I couldn't understand him." My stomach released what it could no longer hold back. I began retching, sobs convulsing me. The child's voice inside my mind wailing, "*he's dying.*"

CHAPTER NINE

"Nest? You're sure?"

When I came back out, Pitts' mom and my friends were gone. The security guard followed me to the elevator. "I'm leaving," I told him.

"I'm going to make sure of it," he said roughly. He rode with me to the lobby. When the doors opened, he warned, "Don't come back."

Pitts and Diddleman ran over as soon as he was gone. "Man," Diddleman exclaimed. "What happened in there?"

"Where's your mom?" I asked Pitts.

"I'm not sure. She said she would handle things."

I thought it was Dr. Potter who went for security. Could Pitts' mom have gotten them? Did she also believe it wasn't my dad? Could

I have been that wrong? No. It was him. I didn't know what was going on, but I knew I had to think things through before doing anything else.

The sky was clear but it was so humid you could swipe your hand through the air and it'd come back wet. We walked over to my house and were pitted out by the time we got there. As we walked, I told them what had happened in the room. I started crying again, blubbering like a baby. Diddleman kept his hand on my shoulder. Even when I stopped crying, he still continued to leave it there.

"Alive? Boggs? Nest?" Pitts asked, tears also welling behind his glasses.

"I think he was trying to tell me my sister and mom are still alive." I said. "He found them."

"But why Boggs? Nest?"

I shook my head.

"It was him," Diddleman said. He squeezed. "I bet it was him."

I thought he was saying he shared the idea, it was my dad But he was talking about Teddy.

The yard looked bare and deserted. The camping gear dad and I had been using, gone. The doors to the house stood wide open. When we went in, we found stuff from drawers tossed out onto the floor, food smeared on the walls, furniture missing, the television gone. Spray-paint on the living room wall in large, red letters read WHY US NOT YOU?

My parents had lived in this house since Shilo and I were born. Our neighbors weren't just the people we lived next to, they were family. We knew which of them had marital problems, children who got in trouble, and those who were old and lonely because their children moved away. At night when it was too warm to stay inside, neighbors came out onto front porches. Men would raise their hands in salutes to one another. Those taking an evening walk would stop by for a glass of tea or a beer, or just stop by and sit on the steps to rest before moving along. Mrs. Cox across the street brought over cookies whenever she made too many to eat, or mom would take a batch to them.

"Man, they wiped you out," Diddleman began walking around, picking things off the floor, checking to see if what was left was anything interesting before dropping it back into the mess. "This is worse than Pitts' room."

"Who would do this?" I stared at the wording. It was hard to believe anyone outside the neighborhood would have done this either. "How the heck do I know why we weren't hit?"

We went through the each of the rooms downstairs before going up. My parents' room appeared no different. Shilo's room, too, had been ransacked. Seeing all their clothes thrown on the floor, the mattresses of their beds gone, windows bare of curtains, gave me such a heavy sense of loss. It felt like gazing at a graveyard, something missing, lost, empty. Dry sobs trembled out of me. I had no more tears left.

"You okay, Jake?" Pitts came up behind me.

"Yeah." I wasn't, but he knew that.

"Come on. You need to see this?"

"What?" I didn't think I could take anymore. I wanted to run. Run from the house, my father dying, my mother and sister gone, run fast and far as if by running I could move back time. If I hadn't gone for a haircut, would that have changed anything? If I hadn't, I wouldn't have seen Sheriff Boggs come into the shop looking for Officer Wilcox. I wouldn't have gone for lunch and got so curious. Pitts may not have Yahoo'd for any more UFO information. I'd have been home when the storm hit. Kept Shilo's secret. She might have come home before the storm. Before…

"You won't want to miss this." Pitts jarred me back to the present.

I let myself be led to my room. I stopped, stunned. My computer was setting on my desk along with my X-Box controls. The coin bottle where I put the change from my pockets every night was still half-full. My bed made, something I did before dad and I moved out to the tent. On the bed, half tented was the *Counterfeit Son*, the novel I'd been reading.

"What the hell?" Diddleman came up behind Pitts and me. "This is freaky."

"We need to call the police," Pitts said.

We were standing on the porch waiting for the police to come.

"Look, isn't that Templeton?" Diddleman pointed across the street. Teddy Templeton sat in a webbed lawn chair with his legs crossed, relaxing. He wasn't wearing his Cardinals hat. Instead, he was wearing a yellow cap with a black bill and in the center of the cap, a large black "I." It was my University of Iowa baseball cap.

"Hey Teddy." I jumped off the porch and headed over. "I need to talk to you."

Teddy took off running. He was quick.

I chased him around the ruined yards, across decrepit blocks, to houses and life untouched. He was fast, much faster than me. My lungs hurt. My gut clenched. Sweat rolled off me. I could hear Pitts and Diddleman somewhere behind yelling, but I didn't want to slow down to wait for them. I needed to know why my room, in all of the house, hadn't been touched by whoever robbed us. I wanted to know what Teddy was doing there, and why he took my hat.

I was three or four blocks over from my street when I lost sight of him for a minute, then spotted him peeking around the corner of a house, as if he was waiting for me to catch up. Like we were playing some sort of game. By the time I reached the point where he'd been, he was gone. But the gate to the backyard was open. I ran in that direction and found Teddy in the very back, stopped by a chain-link fence. "Ted...dy...hold...up." I couldn't catch my breath.

Teddy waved.

"I'm not mad. I just want to know what you saw. Who did that to our house? You?"

"There he is," Diddleman shouted, coming up puffing behind me.

"Man's he's fast." Pitts coughed his words.

My eyes moved from Teddy to the hand he was holding in the air as if to wave again. His left hand. I saw the abnormality of his index finger being much longer than his middle finger. "Jakob," Teddy called, his voice high pitched. "I'll take you. Come." He waved for me to go to him.

Diddleman pushed past me, his upper body leaning slightly forward in a tackle position.

Teddy glanced at him then back to me. Then with what looked like no effort at all, he took a step and leaped away from Diddleman, flying over the fence, clearing the six-foot height by at least six inches.

Diddleman stumbled and fell. "Get back here, you freak."

Pitts and I ran over. "You okay?" I helped him up.

"That guy's totally weird. He's the one who robbed you. Wasn't that your hat?"

"He couldn't have taken everything," Pitts argued.

The three of us stared across the fence. Teddy had disappeared.

"He's one of them." Diddleman choked, then he leaned over and retched.

"Diddleman, you okay?"

"Yeah, yeah. Man it's hot."

"If Templeman didn't leave the message in your living room, he knows who did."

"I don't think he wants to talk to us," I agreed.

"Where did he want you to go?"

"How would I know. Come on. Let's get back to the house. Forget Templeton. He can have my hat."

By the time we got back over onto my block, a police car was parked at the curb. Seeing us, Officer Hayworth got out of his car, situated his cap making sure the bill was straight and shifted his duty belt and gun high on his hips. "You've had some trouble, Jake?"

"It was Templeton," Diddleman yelled. "We almost caught him."

I hushed Diddleman and whispered to Pitts. "Forget Teddy."

"Where's your father, Jake?" Officer Hayworth asked. "I'll need to go over what happened with him."

I hesitated. Should I tell him about finding my Dad in the hospital? How at this moment, I had no idea whether he was dead or still alive. I heard my father whisper, "Boggs." Even though I'd known Officer Hayworth all my life, I suddenly felt like I couldn't trust anybody. Except for maybe Sheriff Boggs.

I told Officer Hayworth I wasn't sure. He pulled a small notebook and pen out of his shirt pocket and wrote something down. "Well, I'll give things a look-over and get back to him."

CHAPTER TEN

The light coming in from the window caused the writing to scream off the wall.

"Damn kids." Officer Hayworth scribbled on his writing pad. "Give me an idea of what's missing."

I looked hopelessly around a room vacant of furniture and most anything else valuable. "Everything."

He sniffed, the tip of his tongue popping out to lick his lips. He put his writing pad away then stood with his hands on his hips giving the room and its message a good scrutiny. He slapped his belt as if to make sure of its placement. "I'd better investigate."

I followed him through each of the downstairs rooms. He opened doors to find gutted cupboards. His bird-eyes peeped into drawers where some of the contents hung out like intestines from slit bodies.

"Yep. Looks like you've been cleaned out all right?" He sniffed and shifted his belt. "Hard to figure anyone around here would do something like this, but I always say, when bad things happen, people don't always muster up and do the right thing. They forget the nature of tornadoes."

"The nature?"

"Now let me tell you, there are about two thousand tornadoes sighted each and every year. Most people don't keep track, but I do. It's a hobby of mine." He scratched the side of his nose.

He went on. "Yes sir, most folks think funnels pop out and hit a community once in a life time. But let me tell you," he sniffed again, "I should've been a meteorologist. It's as important as police work. People plan their lives around the weather."

He placed his hand on the butt of his gun in its holster. "You know, I once read about a Nebraska town that was hit year after year for three years, like they were marked on a map. People came up missing and never found. Then there was a community in Kansas. You wouldn't see the town if you were traveling down the road and blinked your eyes, but it was hit twice in one year."

He shifted his duty belt and sniffed, then looked off towards the door leading to the living room. "This isn't the first to hit Pinkerton, not in my lifetime. You probably weren't born yet, it was about fifteen years ago. We were hit by an EF-2. That's the rating those of us who talk about tornadoes use. It means the winds were pretty bad, well over a hundred. It hit down right before the park and came towards town like it meant business. It missed Pinkterton by an inch, but it destroyed the Sterner farm. Pigs and cows found three miles away. Roy and Janie Sterner were killed. Did some damage to your grandparents' farm, too."

He got my attention. I'd spent many a summer night at my grandparents' sitting inside the screened-in back porch listening to the frogs croak down at the pond and the cicadas rub their wings.

"How'd it go from Eagles to Grandpa Muller's without hitting the town?" Grandpa and Grandma Muller lived less than a mile north of Pinkerton.

"Not Reb Muller, your mother's folks. This was on your dad's side. He was born in Royce Martin's place. Didn't you know that, boy?"

I shook my head. Dad had never talked about his parents much. They'd died before I was born.

"I'd have thought he would have mentioned that tornado. He was old enough to remember. It came right past their house. Picked up the hog barn, hogs in it. But not a single shingle blown off the roof."

Office Hayworth sniffed and shifted his belt. "Might as well show me the rest of the house. I'll write a report in case your folks had insurance." He walked out of the kitchen.

I heard him talking to Pitts and Diddleman before I heard steps on the stairs. By the time I reached the landing, all three had come to my room and stood inside the doorway. Had Pitts taken him to my room, first? Officer Hayworth's cap was off and he was scratching his head. "Damnedest thing I ever seen."

Diddleman walked over to the computer. He moved the mouse. The computer flickered on and words appeared on the white screen: FOLLOW ME.

"Who wrote that?" Hayworth asked.

I shook my head. "I don't know."

"Did you do this?" He pointed to the computer, his finger shaking with accusation. As if the message on the computer explained everything being gone in the house. But the screen didn't say where or who to follow, or that the person who left the message took our things.

I couldn't believe he thought I had. "No."

He stared over at Diddleman then turned to Pitts. His eyes bugged. They ended back on me. His voice moved up an octave. "Are you aware I can arrest you for this?"

"For what?" Pitts demanded. "We didn't do anything."

Diddleman raised both hands in the air, surrendering. "I didn't do anything. I touched the mouse by accident. I swear."

"You can't screw around with the police." Officer Hayworth twisted on his heels and started off down the hallway. "Damn kids. As if we aren't busy enough without false alarms."

"He really thought we staged this?" Pitts asked, incredulous.

"Follow me," Diddleman repeated. "Sounds like a line from a horror movie. You know, like someone says follow me and everyone watching knows that it's the one thing *not* to do."

Pitts asked me, "Templeton, do you think?"

I nodded. Who else would have done it?

CHAPTER ELEVEN

When we reached Pitts' house, his parents weren't home. Michael Jackson's *Thriller* was pounding a beat from upstairs. We found Jimmy in his room with the stereo turned heavy bass, full volume.

"Jimmy?" Pitts yelled. "Where's mom?"

"Work." Jimmy yelled back. Then getting up off his bed, he turned the music down.

If asked to bet if Jimmy and Pitts were brothers, no one would take the bet. They looked nothing alike. Four years apart, Pitts' hair was jet black and he ran a comb through it maybe once a day. Jimmy's was sandy-brown, routinely combed with a slip of hair carefully positioned to fall loosely on his forehead.

Jimmy also had lake-blue eyes, but a larger frame with biceps that squeezed the arms of his t-shirt. A girl's dream. Pitts hardly ever talked about girls, and if he looked at the magazines Jimmy slipped to us, he never acknowledged it. He was far more interested in cubing, science, math puzzles.

Jimmy walked over. "You guys horny again? Didn't I supply you with enough porn for the summer?" His forehead slightly furled and his eyes narrowed. "What do you want with mom? Money? You guys in some sort of trouble? I heard dad talking to her on the phone. He sounded upset."

Pitts then told him what happened at the hospital.

"That's bull crap. Why would they be trying to keep Jake from his dad?"

"Exactly," Pitts returned. Pitts then gave him a synopsis of our alien-storm theory.

Jimmy laughed. "Olie, I'm getting worried about you. You're losing it, man."

But Pitts wasn't intimidated. He went on, telling him about what we saw at Eagles Park, specifically the deer, and what I'd seen at Royce Martin's. "Do any of those things sound like we're losing it?"

"Nah, you're the scientist in the family. But can you *prove* it?"

Pitts became angry. "Just because it hasn't been proven doesn't mean it doesn't exist."

"No," Jimmy agreed. "But I've got a few more years on me, and more schooling, too. I've taken a few science classes. In all of them, I haven't heard or read anything about aliens. Comics and paperbacks, now there's another story. Where you getting all this from, Storyman?"

He pointed to me. He took hold of the bedroom door. "You guys better knock it off before you do get in trouble."

He swung the door closed.

"Asshole," Diddleman said.

"Shut up, Diddleman," Pitts moved past us and went into his own room. He went straight over to his chair, picked up his cube and angrily began twisting and turning.

"So what now?" Diddleman whined. "Are we staying here? I'm hungry."

I didn't move beyond Pitts' doorway. "Maybe I should leave. Your mom might be really mad at me."

"She wasn't mad," Pitts said, not looking up from the cube. "She didn't even follow us to the lobby."

"But Jimmy said…"

"Who's listening to him?"

"When do you think she'll be home?" I asked.

Pitts stopped cubing and thought a minute. "About seven."

"I'm going back."

"Can we stop at the Queen?" Diddleman asked.

"I think my dad's dying and I want to see if he did find my mom and sister," I told Pitts. "Maybe he can tell me more. "

"We'll go with you." Pitts stood up.

"No." I held up a hand. "If I'm caught, this time I could get in trouble. Something *is* going on. They kept saying the guy wasn't my dad, like I wouldn't be able to recognize him. And they didn't want to let me see him."

I'm not going to let them know I'm there. I'm sneaking in." I hadn't come up with a plan or anything, but I knew what I had to do."

"We're going." Pitts came over beside me.

"We are?" Diddleman questioned.

"Jake's right," Pitts said. "Something isn't right. My mom wasn't angry at us, but she also was mad and not acting normal, either. She wanted to get rid of us, fast. I want to know why, and she's the only one who can tell us."

We didn't go through the lobby this time. We went through the back door from the parking lot where the nurses and doctors usually parked. Then we took the stairs to the second floor. No one was at the second floor nurses' station desk except for Ashley.

"Pitts, wait." I stopped him from moving into the corridor. "I don't want to chance us getting caught. Maybe Ashly's the one who called security. If she saw me again, she might…"

"So what's the plan?"

A nurse came by, and Pitts quickly closed the door. We waited a couple of minutes. Then he cracked it open again. He listened, then stuck his head out, checking both ways. "Clear."

I whispered. "I'm going straight to my dad's room."

"Okay. I'll try to find my mom."

"What'll I do?" Diddleman asked.

"You stay here. And keep quiet. If Ashley sees only me, then she won't be suspicious something's up."

Pitts canvased the corridor again, "Okay, Jake. Go."

I slipped out, hurrying down the corridor as much as I dared, not wanting to catch anyone's notice. It was the closest patient hall, opposite the one dad was on, but I knew this one circled around to his.

I acted as naturally as I could, keeping my eyes steady on one opened doorway after another, ready to slip into the closest one if I saw either the nurse that had been in my dad's room or Dr. Potter.

It was late in the afternoon but before dinner. The corridor stayed empty. I got to my dad's room quickly. I opened the door carefully, an inch at a time, taking what seemed like hours before I got it open enough to see if anyone was with him. Then I opened it up fully.

It was empty. The bed neatly made. The heart monitoring machine, gone. Blood pressure machine, IVs, gone.

"Can I help you?"

I swung around. A nurse stood holding a medicine tray. I thought quickly. "I'm here to visit my grandmother, Agnus Muller."

"You must have the wrong room," she said. "Muller. I don't remember a Muller being registered for this floor. Let's go up to the front desk. I could be wrong. I just came back on schedule. I was off for a couple of days."

I followed her as she headed down the corridor, back towards the nurse's station saying, "That was a horrible storm that came through, wasn't it? The tornado didn't hit our neighborhood, but we lost three trees from the wind."

Then on cat feet, I began back-stepping for every step she took forward. I slipped inside the opened doorway of 228, across the hall from where dad had been. An older man lay in bed watching the early evening news. Before he noticed me, I slipped behind the door.

The nurse's voice quieted. Then I heard steps coming back. I held my breath. She went as far as the short corridor, and she must have looked for me there. When she didn't see me, she came back, seemly undisturbed. Why not? Visitors probably got in the wrong room all the time. And I didn't look like a trouble maker.

I came out from behind the door.

"What you doing there, boy?" The old man wasn't watching the news any longer.

I side-stepped his question. "I must have the wrong room."

"No rooms behind that door." He raised onto his elbow and his free hand moved as if to pick up his call button for a nurse.

"Okay, I was hiding. I went into the wrong room and I didn't want to get in trouble." I held my arms out to my sides, palms up. Nothing to hide here. "I was going to visit my grandmother."

"Which room?"

The early evening news didn't seem too different from what the news had been in the last few days. I heard, "...turbulent weather." The man acted as if he had been already adequately informed and unaffected. My coming into his room was far more interesting.

"The one across the hall," I answered him.

He shook his head. "Then you got the wrong room for sure. There was a man in that room, not a woman."

"You sure?"

"They brought him in a couple of nights ago. Middle of the night. Poor bastard was in bad shape."

I moved closer to him, wanting to keep our voices low. "When did they move him? Was he?"

"Dead? Nah, I don't think so. Sheet wasn't over his head. IV tubes still stuck in him."

His eyes were so faded and watery, I was surprised he could see me. His gray-horned eyebrows rose. "You the kid they threw out this mornin'?"

I didn't answer.

"Did you know the guy?"

I nodded. My own eyes beginning to water. "Yes."

He worried his mouth, then said, "Wasn't much after they threw you out that the doctor came back in with some security men and moved him."

"Did you catch where they took him?"

He shook his head. His mouth worried again. "Maybe transferred him to another hospital."

"Yeah. Maybe." But my gut didn't settle with the idea of them worrying about his health. My gut said they'd moved him because Dr. Potter thought he told me something. Something I wasn't supposed to know.

CHAPTER TWELVE

When I met up with Pitts in the stairwell, he said Ashley told him his mom wasn't feeling well and had gone home. "She thought I knew because she said my mom left soon after I did."

"My dad's gone, too." I told them about finding the room empty and what the man in room 228 said he saw.

Pitts shook his head. "None of this makes sense. Why would they move him and why is everyone being so secretive?"

"I don't know. Let's go back to your place."

When we got back to the Pitts' house, Jimmy was leaving. "Got a date." He finger combed back his hair at the sides and pulled slightly to make sure the curl was still in place.

"Mom came home after you left. She and dad. She said for you guys to call for pizza and to tell you that they wouldn't be home for a while."

"Where'd they go?" Pitts asked.

"Didn't say."

"Did she seem…sick?"

Jimmy gave him an annoyed look. "Why would she be sick?"

"She came home from work."

"Yeah, but she wasn't sick. She said she and dad had an appointment they forgot." Then he pulled up, changing from his parents to us. "Hey, what are you guys doin'? You sure you're not in trouble?"

"Have fun on your date," Pitts said.

"Plan to." He passed us, but not before punching Diddleman on the arm and saying, "Stay out of my room."

"What'll we do now?" Diddleman asked, rubbing the punch.

Pitts and I exchanged looks. Pitts said, "Wait for my mom, I guess."

Diddleman suggested ordering pizza. He ate most of it while Pitts and I went over everything, from the storm, my dad missing, then to showing up at the hospital, our house vandalized, Teddy.

He stopped me when I recalled chasing Teddy. I slipped and mentioned that Teddy wanted me to follow him. "I thought you said Templeton didn't say anything."

I'd forgotten the lie. I tried to cover myself. "I wasn't sure. He might have said something like 'come on.' I guess he wanted me to follow him."

Diddleman garbled, his mouth full of stuffed-crust. "That's what it said on your computer. Follow me. The freak did it. Told you."

"We need to find Templeton," Pitts and I chorused.

"Let's wait until my mom gets home. She'll tell us what happened at the hospital," he said.

But when his parents got home, they seemed upset, like they'd had an argument or something. His mom complained about the pizza mess in the kitchen. His dad asked if we had nothing else to do but sit around doing nothing. Pitts pointed out it was after ten and then asked his mom about the hospital and why she'd come home. Was she sick? And I added that I'd gone back and my dad wasn't in his room.

She turned and stared at me. "You boys went back to the hospital?"

I glanced for help from Pitts.

"Jake knows it was his dad, no matter what anyone else is saying. He's right, isn't he?"

"Who saw you?" His mom exchanged a worried look with his dad.

"No one," Pitts answered.

"No one? You're sure?" His dad asked, giving me a scorching stare.

Pitts must have felt like he needed to say something, so he answered. "Well, Ashley. But it was just me and she told me mom went home sick."

His mom's tone softened but you could tell she was just as concerned. "You were there, right Jake? You had to of been to say the room was empty."

I couldn't lie to his mom. "Yes, but the only one who saw me was a nurse. She didn't know who I was, and when she caught me in the room, I told her I was looking for my grandmother. She just thinks I got the wrong room."

Pitts' mother seemed relieved but still skeptical.

"The guy in the room across the hall also saw me," I added.

"What guy? Mr. Lyle?"

"I don't know his name. An old guy. Real old. Bushy eyebrows."

"And you told him who you were?"

"No. But he guessed I was who they threw out of the room this morning." I went on with the rest of it. "He told me they moved my dad right after I was gone."

Again worried exchanges were made.

Why were they still acting like it wasn't?

"It's my dad. I know it's him. And…he's really hurt."

They still both denied my dad had been in the room. "You're mistaken, Jake," she said. "The patient's name was Lawrence Denazell. He wasn't on the register because they were transferring him to a burn unit at Iowa City. I'm sorry we got your hopes up."

She was lying.

"I went with your mother to see Dr. Potter," Pitts' dad added. "He explained everything to us."

They were lying.

Still, they warned all of us from going back to the hospital.

"School's going to start in a week. Enjoy the rest of your summer," Pitts' dad said.

We went upstairs. Pitts was especially quiet. He had to have known they were lying, too. How could I have mistaken this Lawrence guy as my dad? And why would my dad have told me my mom and sister were alive, somewhere at Eagles. Nest?

Diddleman pulled a sleeping bag out of the hoard and curled up on the floor. Pitts cubed for a while, then he eventually crawled into bed. It was getting late. It was almost midnight before I lay down.

I was tired. The type of tired where every movement seems like an effort. But not sleepy. My mind was running like a horse once the gate had open. Nest? Nest? Then it came to me. My dad was telling me where he'd seen my mom and sister. A place where only I would know.

When I jumped to the ground, I heard Pitts. "Jake, here, catch this."

He threw something. I caught it. A flashlight. He climbed down the trellis on the side of the house like a spider canvassing its web. Then Diddleman came to the window and threw a bundle of clothes. "In case it rains," Pitts explained.

Diddleman jumped the last bit with a huge thump and stumbled to the ground. He jumped up with both arms high above his head. "I'm okay."

"Shhh," Pitts warned. "My mom is a light sleeper."

"You guys don't have to come with me." I didn't want them in trouble as well as my possibly getting myself in deep Dutch.

"Going," Pitts said. He untied the bundle. He threw each of us a hooded shirt.

It didn't look like rain. It was still warm. A three-quarter moon held bright-white in the summer night's sky.

We tied the shirts around our waists, then went to our bikes, walking them away from the house before jumping on. When we were a safe distance from the house, Pitts stopped. "Where to? Back to the hospital?"

I shook my head. "Eagles."

"Eagles?" Diddleman protested. "In the dark?"

I told them what I remembered and how I thought my dad was trying to tell me where I could find my mom and sister.

Pitts seemed hesitant. "Eagles is a big place, Jake."

"He said 'Nest.' Between him and me that could only be one place. When we all went to the Kennedy Space Center, he took me to show me an eagle's nest."

"A rocket?" Diddleman questioned. "I thought your dad wasn't an astronaut."

"He's not, he's an engineer. It's his responsibility to make sure the crew gets back safe. This was a real eagle and a real nest, not the launch pad. Dad said that eagles had been nesting in it long before man headed to space. Each and every year they came back. And there was one in it that day. We watched. The eagle stood and positioned itself on the rim of the nest and then it opened its wings and launched. It was cool."

I let the moment be for a few minutes. It was the first time dad had taken all of us, mom, Shilo and me, with him to Cape Canaveral. I remembered how proud I was that everyone knew him. Respected him. Would I continue to remember my dad the way he was that day? Young? Healthy? Excited to school me at the eagles' nest? Not Shilo, just him and me, as if it would always be our moment.

"I've seen it happen twice," I recounted. "Once at the Cape and once at Eagles Park."

Pitts said, "And you think you can find this place? In the dark?"

"It's close to our fishing hole. I've been there dozens of times. There's a cabin not far from it, and sometimes, when I was little and if dad was only around for a little while, having to go back to base, we'd go up for overnight."

Diddleman wasn't buying it. "I don't know you guys. It's dark. And it might start storming."

Pitts gave the clouds a good scrutiny. Then he made up his mind. "Let's go."

It was super quiet as we biked through town. If we saw any headlights, the one in the lead was to veer over and stop. We couldn't risk being caught by the police. If they spotted us, we'd have been sent back home, having broken curfew.

The highway was just as vacant, giving the warning that we could get run over no credence. And the three-quarter moon in a cloudless sky offered light.

Eyes blinked from the shoulder of the road. Once something scuttled across in front of me. A raccoon, maybe. It didn't stop to ask where we were off to and we didn't stop to check out if it was a raccoon or maybe a large possum. There was no stopping now.

The camping parking lot was at least a mile from the main entrance. I expected the camp to be full, but there was a huge sign barring entrance: "CAMP CLOSED."

"What do you think?" I asked Pitts.

"Probably because of Officer Wilcox," he guessed. "They may have closed the whole park."

"Still," I warned Diddleman. "Be careful. We don't want anyone to know we're here."

The road curled through large, spreading oaks. At the small registration kiosk, a police car was parked. We had to pass it to get to the trail to take us where my dad and I used to fish.

I waved the guys over and got off my bike. "Stay under the trees. Move slow."

Pitts and Diddleman followed suit. We walked our bikes across the entrance way. Several times, I thought we were had. I thought I heard someone call out. I found out why we weren't caught once we got up closer to the kiosk. The cop was in his car, music low, his body leaning, head lying on the opened window. Asleep.

Still, no matter how slowly we moved, it sounded like our tires crunched every fallen leaf. Our feet hit and set rolling each and every fallen acorn or rock.

We didn't get back on our bikes until we were well past and around a bend. We traveled past camping lots that provided electric for RVs, room for a tent, a fire pit...all empty and ghostlike. Going past one lot, I thought I saw someone, but then figured it must have been a shadow or maybe a deer. It was the cool thing about camping at Eagles. The deer were so used to people, you'd wake to find them grazing on grass next to your tent.

We came to the place where a trail moved off the road. A small wood arrow read in white, painted letters: "Summit Trail 2.5 miles."

"Hide the bikes," I told them.

"How far?" Pitts asked.

"The trail goes up and meets with a bridle trail that goes to the very top of this ridge. That's the way to the summit. But this trail goes back down to the lake.

"How far?" Diddleman wanted to know. "Two miles"

"Two, maybe three miles to the lake," I told him.

"Geezzz…"

"You don't have to go, Diddleman. You can stay here with our bikes. Make sure no one steals them."

Diddleman glanced around at the emptiness. "Who's going to steal them? No one's here."

"The cop might wake up and start driving around."

"Yeah, another reason why I'm not staying." He looked up to the heavens. "Why me?"

Nothing answered him.

Pitts and I didn't wait for him to ask more questions. Pitts clicked the flashlight on. We took the trail, Pitts with the flashlight in the lead. We walked in a single line, not talking. There really wasn't much to say. I walked with sure steps for a ways, then as the trees started canceling the added light from the moon, I began to doubt whether I could find the exact spot where dad and I had seen the eagle's nest.

I was seven or eight at the time. There might not even be a nest anymore. But if the eagles kept coming back where rockets launched, in all that noise, I figured there was a good chance an eagle might return to a quiet, peaceful place like this. Besides, it was the only explanation I could come up with for the term "Nest."

"Hearing acute." It was a line from Poe that popped in my mind. I didn't completely understand it at its reading but it made sense now. I could hear everything. A leaf could be heard tumbling through branches. Fireflies blinked on and off in empty spaces. The hoot of an owl. The soft thump of an acorn hitting the ground. The fluttering of bats' wings or maybe just a night bird moving off to another tree.

The air became close, smelling of dust, dying oak leaves, decay.

"Hold it." Pitts stopped short. He moved the flashlight beam around the bushes off the trail. "I see someone."

I looked ahead on the trail. I didn't see anything.

"Sorry," he said, moving the light back to the trail. "It must have been a deer. Let's go." He stepped forward, and just as he did, something did move. All of us heard something push past and move branches.

"Jesus," Diddleman gasped.

"Shhh."

But Diddleman was too afraid to be quieted. "We should have gone to the police. Didn't your dad say to tell Sheriff Boggs?"

"No," I whispered back. "I have to find them. Go back if you want."

"Guys, quiet." Pitts warned both of us. Pitts turned off the light.

"What are you doing?" Diddleman coarsely whispered. "Now we can't see where it is."

Pitts whispered back. "And it can't see us."

We waited.

"Maybe it's a bear? Or mountain lion?" Diddleman

"There aren't any bears or mountain lions," I whispered.

"Sure. That's what the bears and mountain lions want you to think."

"You were right, Pitts, it probably was just a deer," I said. "Come on."

I took the lead. Pitts turned the flashlight back on and zeroed the beam ahead on the trail.

We went cautiously, and when we got to the spot, we stopped, seeing three or four white-tailed deer off to the side of the trail, under the trees, standing like statues, mouths chewing contentedly but their eyes just as big and round as ours must have been. All of us sighed with relief. We continued, walking more briskly and confidently.

When we finally got to the crossing bridle trail, we came out in the open. The trees were cut back. Limbs pruned so riders wouldn't be knocked off their horses. The light from the moon was completely gone. I looked up. Clouds had come in.

"Okay, we go straight," I said.

Pitts, too, must have begun to doubt me. "It's gonna get worse if it starts to rain. Why don't we come back tomorrow, daylight."

"I can't risk it. What if they've been hurt like my dad?"

He shined the flashlight beam over where the trail picked up.

"We go home once we get to the lake. If you haven't found the place by then, I agree with Diddleman, we need to get help. We'll go back and convince my mom and dad. Or, like your father said, we'll tell Sheriff Boggs."

"Okay." I had to agree to it. If we got clear to the lake and I hadn't seen where to turn off from the trail, then I had to admit I would be wrong. And what I hadn't told Pitts and Diddleman was that we never went to the cabin or the place we fished from this direction. We went from the lake's side. I thought it better not to risk going from that way because we'd have to get past the entrance and the parking lot. The cops on night shift could spot us. I hadn't planned on someone keeping tabs on the camping area. It was just luck he fell asleep.

We continued, still in a single line. With only a small beam of light to lead us and the brush and trees creating a black wall, what started to feel like a labyrinth path twisted and turned, moving toward the lake. Tree roots tried to trip us. A rumbling of thunder shook our nerves. Trees grew taller, branches hung like low heavy arms. Owl hooting suddenly sounded more human. *Who? Who?* A leaf crashed through branches. Acorns struck the ground. Fireflies morphed into blinking eyes; watching, calculating, appearing, disappearing. The air churned with dust from the bushes and trees, and as we moved around and through, it became difficult to breathe.

Then I spotted a small break in the flashlight's beam. It was another trail, unmarked, moving off this one. "We go this way," I whispered. Although why we continued to whisper I don't know. There was no one around us to hear.

"Off the trail?" Diddleman choked.

"You sure?" Pitts asked.

"Yeah," I lied. Hoping it wasn't a lie.

CHAPTER THIRTEEN

Was I scared? Hell, yes.

If I was wrong, we could get lost. More lost than we might already be. If I was right, if this led us to the place where dad and I found the eagle's nest, what would I find? Would there still be a cabin? Who had my mom and sister? If they were alive, they had to be trapped or held prisoner. My heart tickled like a bomb close to triggering its blast.

The trail became narrow. Bushes and branches pushed harder to keep us out, ripping at our skin, snagging our clothes. Thunder rumbled again. Raindrops. Diddleman started complaining louder. Pitts again began second-guessing me. Still I kept moving forward, keeping in my mind the tree where I had seen the nest, the eagle standing up, and in one swift and glorious movement launching up into the sky, rising higher and higher and higher.

Yet, unlike the eagle, my mind echoed each and every comment Pitts and Diddleman made. I began to have an off feeling, with each step I took forward, blindly moving to a place remembered but not known. I was sinking lower and lower, saying goodbye. Not to family and friends, but to who I had been. Because if I survived, I felt like I would no longer be Jake Cahill.

It began to rain harder. We stopped and put on our shirts, hooding our heads. The deeper we moved into the woods, the more I knew it couldn't have been aliens that took my mom and sister. The entire idea of aliens from another planet sounded stupid now. A spaceship couldn't have flown through these woods, I realized. And how would the aliens know about the camping cabin? Why would they have come to where the eagle nested?

And wasn't the eagle's nest closer to the lake. It didn't seem like dad and I had walked this far when he saw it flying. Aliens. Man, we were as dumb as little kids. And me? Hell, my imagination conjured up Diddleman's lions and bears leaping out at every bush I passed. Why would aliens have picked up my mom and sister? Because my dad worked for NASA?

Then I thought I heard something. A muted cry. I stopped. Listened. Nothing.

"Did you guys hear something?"

"Yeah, like my stomach growling," Diddleman answered.

It was one thing for me to get lost and maybe never find my way back. I pushed back what seemed like the thousandth brush. To follow a clue and maybe end up like my dad. Was he still alive? Dead? What had happened to him? How could I have let Pitts and Diddleman come with me?

I stepped over the hundredth root.

Pitts planned to go to UI where his brother was going. He wanted us to room together. Diddleman may have had trouble at home, but that didn't mean his folks didn't love him.

Something moved again. Closer.

They had someone to live for. I had no one. My mom and sister could be dead. Dad may have found them alive, but that didn't mean they still were. Maybe they had got trapped in the fire, too.

Movement to my left.

"I may have gotten this all wrong. You guys go back. In the morning, tell Sheriff Boggs what my dad said."

"You aren't going alone," Pitts said.

Even Diddleman said, "One for all and all for one."

CHAPTER FOURTEEN

*T*wo things abruptly changed. A smell of charred wood and a heavy, rotten smell, like meat forgotten on the counter on a hot day.

"There." I pointed. This time I wasn't mistaken. Someone was following us.

"Where? I don't see anything." Pitts panned the beam around everywhere.

I flipped off my hood to see better. Rain dripped off my eyelashes. I hadn't been wrong. This was where we camped. I was almost sure of it. I headed around Pitts, out of the flashlight's security and into the dark, pushing quickly through, no longer worrying about the scratching. I heard Pitts and Diddleman not far behind me. They moved just as quickly, feet thumping on the hard ground.

I came to a clearing. My eyes adjusted. It was lighter with the walls of darkness gone. Still dark, but I could make out a figure squatting on the ground.

"It's Templeton, man." When Diddleman screamed the name, the figure stood up.

It was smaller than Templeton. About half his size. What was it?

It was too dark to make out its features, but it had large eyes and it screamed a high pitch, *SQUEAL!*

"Let's get him." Diddleman pushed past me.

We were again on the chase, jumping over tree trunks, standing water, shoving aside branches. This time not in someone's backyard. No longer on any path.

We slowed down. Pitts' flashlight caught a deer laying on the ground. The light moved across its body, it's gut open, intestines scattered out and across its hide. Moving up to it, the light pulled larger to where we could see the grayish-blue entrails, small, making a round pile on the ground. White rib bones cracked, standing high and wide. Red meat. Dried red blood.

"Jesus," Diddleman prayed, his voice a quivering whisper.

"What was it?" I asked Pitts, meaning what we were chasing.

"I'm not sure," Pitts said. "It didn't look human. No bigger than a boy. Did you see its arms, they hung almost to the ground."

"Could it be an alien? Were we right after all?

"This ain't no E.T." Diddleman said. "Let's go home."

"You guys go."

"You aren't thinking of still following it?"

"It may lead me to my mom."

"But," Diddleman said, "that means she could also be…"

"Shut up, Diddleman," Pitts demanded. "Go back. I'm staying with Jake." He knelt by the deer. "When you hear about this, stuff like cattle mutilations, you never picture something like this." He reached out, stroking the deer's neck. "You were right, nothing like E.T., but if there is bad in our world, there could also be bad in theirs. I never thought of it before. But it's logical. And guys, I don't think this deer was dead when it tore it open."

"How do you know?" Diddleman choked.

"It's not very logical. I just got a feeling."

"Let's go." I started off, but Pitts stopped me.

"Jake, promise me. If we don't find your mom and sister in a little bit, then we go back and tell the police."

I headed off again, not agreeing or disagreeing, but wanting whatever it was not to get very far so that we couldn't follow.

But as we continued on in the direction it'd gone, we discovered another deer, then another. One had antlers. A doe. Two small fawns, white dots almost gone on their butchered hides. The woods became a war field, man against beast--aliens butchering beasts.

SQUEAL!

"Come on, it's close. Try not to make any noise."

SQUEAL!

It was making the same noise over and over as if calling to us. As if it wanted us to follow it. If we went back, no one would believe us. I'd seen it, and still I was having a hard time believing what I saw. We needed some kind of proof. We had to at least follow it until I figured out exactly where we were. Only then could we bring help back to where we'd again find the slaughter.

Then we pushed out of the woods into another clearing. This one was larger. A burnt out structure stood at its far edge.

You could still smell burning wood although there was no smoke. Was this the cabin? I glanced around, not recognizing anything from my childhood. I listened for the sound of the lake. But it didn't feel close. Had we somehow started moving up, not down?

SQUEAL!

Then we saw it. When Pitts light caught it, it was standing in a pool of blood. What looked like a body lay close to its feet.

SQUEAL!

CHAPTER FIFTEEN

"Shilo? Mom?" I started running. If it was one of them, I was going to kill it.

But the alien was much faster. It was as if it vanished, there one moment and gone the next. The only way I could tell that it existed at all was the bloody footprints it left.

The girl was naked. A gaping hole was open where her stomach should have been. Her guts covered her chest as if someone had taken them out and neatly placed them there. Her ribs, like with the deer, were broken open, cracked pieces of bone, white chards sticking up.

My stomach volcanoed up my throat. The bile hot and bitter. I forced my eyes to her face. A girl. About Shilo's age. Light painted with black streaks of dried blood. Eyes, white, rolled back in her head. And her head thrown back, mouth wide in a scream.

"That's it. We're going for the police," Pitts said.

"Man…oh man…"Diddleman was pacing, retching.

Young like Shilo…but not Shilo.

I swallowed hard.

Pitts squatted down and brushed back her hair from her face. And when he did, I saw the wide cut in her throat. The reason for the bloody pool she lay in. Her head had been cut so deep, her head was almost severed.

I ran to the bushes, retched.

There was very little in my stomach, but I gagged until only yellow bile spilled from my lips. I turned back. Pitts was right. We needed to go get the police.

The girl lay like a dark ruin on an earthy pallet.

Diddleman and Pitts were gone.

I found Pitts walking around the burnt building. I went over, meeting him at what must have once been the entrance. Nothing could be distinguished as having been real or alive.

I glanced around, "Where's Diddleman?"

Pitts looked, too. "He was here a minute ago."

Then the thought that came to both of us struck terror through our souls. Pitts started calling, "Diddleman. Hey, we're going back."

SQUEAL!

It came running around the burned cabin. Its feet pounding hard, coming straight towards us. And with it, ran Chewbaka.

"Chewbaka!"

Tongue hanging out his mouth, he came lobbing over, throwing himself on me, licking.

"Let's get out of here," Pitts yelled. "Come on."

He ran in the direction we'd come from.

"Pitts, look! Chewbaka."

What had been running with him halted.

SQUEAL!

Chewbaka got off me. He stood, staring not at IT, but over at the overgrowth on the other side of the burnt cabin. He growled.

Something larger. It pushed back the brush and stepped out just as Pitts moved past. Pitts fell to the ground.

"Pitts!"

I started to run to him. Then I felt a large blow to my head. Pain ripped through my skull.

CHAPTER SIXTEEN

*I*t smelled moldy and rotten, like taking the garbage can lid off when it's been well over a hundred for a couple of days.

My head felt as if it was going to explode. A cutting stab radiated from my forehead, across my skull, lightning strikes down into my neck. I could feel a wetness dribbling down from my forehead, past the crack of my eye. My mouth tasted something metallic, warm. Blood.

I couldn't move. I found myself hanging against a cold stone wall. My feet and legs were restrained, my hands tied at my waist.

A string of color exploded, one color after another; greens, blues, deep reds and brilliant yellows, gold. They swirled around and around the cave like I was looking through a kaleidoscope. Each time I moved my head, the color patterns changed. Circles, waves of light, bending, arcing into each other, making purple, crimson, stretching from wall to wall, ceiling to floor, bouncing, striking.

A sliver of light from the top of the stone ceiling gave off a narrow bit of light. A rainbow of color moved from it. I was in a cave. But where?

Then I saw the fire. This time the color flared with the flame in the fire ring. The smell of cooked meat made my stomach growl. It smelled good.

And IT.

It sat with its back to me, handling what it was cooking. Small, the size of a child. But its head was much larger than its body. And its skin was gray like the cold stone of the cave.

Pitts? Diddleman? Were they tied up somewhere here, too?

I squinted, trying to see between the streaks of colors, waiting for them to recede in order to focus. That's when I saw the hooded shirts Diddleman and Pitts had been wearing.

They were here. Somewhere. Then I spotted another pile of clothing. On top lay what appeared to be a sky-blue color. Sky-blue, like the blouse my sister had been wearing when she was taken.

I must have moaned. The figure over by the fire stood up and turned around. Large, oval-shaped black eyes stared over at me. It was holding a stick. Bits of what looked like meat strung on it.

Oh my God. Diddleman. Pitts.

It cocked its head.

SQUEAL!

"What have you done with my friends?!" I screamed, struggling against the ropes biting into me. My head thundering.

"DAAIDDDDDIDDA."

It cocked its head again and held out the stick.

Colors flowed from the stick and it. Shades of pink, then yellow.

"Where are my mom and sister?"

"DAAIDDDDDIDIDAWOOOO?" The sound came from a hole where its mouth should have been. No nose. This wasn't human. It stepped forward.

"Don't you come near me."

My body began shaking, trembling uncontrollably. My eyes blinked. Darkness. Then light. Blues, greens, purple. Darkness.

It came closer. So close, I could smell the blood on its body. Blood still smeared on its gray feet. Not feet exactly. Clubs. Hard. They thumped the stone as it came closer.

"Pitts?!" I yelled. "Diddleman?! Mom?!"

It was so close now, I could smell it. A bitterness that itched my nose, a stinging smell of dirt, rot, decay.

It was so close now, I could feel its heat. It brought the stick to my mouth.

"Get away from me."

Its eyes didn't move from side to side. They seemed too large, fixed. But there came an expression in them, as if it was trying to understand me. As if it couldn't figure out why I was so terrified.

Then it raised up what must have been its hand, fingers long. Flashes from black to green, hands black to yellow, black to four long, thin gray fingers, no thumb. And its index finger longer than its middle finger.

Much longer.

"DAAIDDDDIDDAWOOOO."

My eyes warred to stay open. The pounding in my head multiplied. It was going to kill me.

"DAAIDDIDIDDAWOOOOO. JAKKEEEEE."

ABERRANCE

A Criminal Investigation

2016

172

Thanks to you the Reader

Thank you to all who purchased this book and gave their valued leisure time to read it. You are the treasure for any author. If you would like to keep informed on when the second book, *Aberrance*, will be released, please sign up on my website: djadamson.com. Reviews are always appreciated on Amazon.com or Goodreads.com.

D. J. Adamson

While the places where she sets her stories are fictional, D. J. Adamson's family roots grow deep in the Midwest and it is here where she sets much of her work. Along with her husband and two Welsh Terriers, she makes her home in Southern California.

To learn more about D. J. Adamson

Visit her website: http://www.djadamson.com
Or read about her and her enjoyment of reading on Goodreads.

To purchase Outré or *Admit to Mayhem*, the first in her Lillian Dove Mystery series, go to Amazon.com